POWELL'S ARMY

#2 APACHE RAIDERS

BY TERENCE DUNCAN

ZEBRA BOOKS
KENSINGTON PUBLISHING CORP.

ZEBRA BOOKS

are published by

Kensington Publishing Corp.
475 Park Avenue South
New York, NY 10016

Copyright © 1987 by Terence Duncan

All rights reserved. No part of this book may be reproduced in any form or by any means without the prior written consent of the Publisher, excepting brief quotes used in reviews.

First printing: May 1987

Printed in the United States of America

CHAPTER ONE

Gerald Glidinghawk scanned the horizon. It was broken by red bluffs and mesas that tilted crazily into the gorge cut by the Gila San Francisco. He sensed men nearby. Red men, most likely Apache. Chiricahua Apache. Soldiers would have made too much noise, with boots clomping and horsehooves beating like flint against the rock.

He eased himself into a crevice high atop the headland and felt for the knife in his bootlike moccasin. He had his Remington with him, but he hoped he wouldn't have to use it.

Far below, he could see the cold camp he had stealthily circled away from. He had climbed to this vantage point when he first suspected intruders. Strangers of any race out here could only mean trouble.

Cold camp. That was an odd name for a fireless camp, out here in southeastern Arizona. True, they had left no whisps of smoke to announce their presence, but the ground itself radiated heat. The precaution hadn't helped anyway.

Glidinghawk pressed his spine into the rocks and tilted his head. He thought he saw a faint dust trail further up toward the Gila Mountains. Landrum Davis had headed north from camp, to scout out the route they would follow tomorrow. They had tossed a coin on it — a half eagle — and Glidinghawk won. He got to stay with Celia Louise Burnett, to guard the camp.

That was fine. Landrum was as good a scout as any Indian, and more accustomed to the climate than Glidinghawk. Texas was a damned sight more like Arizona than the northern plains where Glidinghawk had grown up.

Glidinghawk was Omaha, a Sioux tribe. Up there, where his people had been herded like cattle into reservations, it was Choke-Cherry month. Glidinghawk wondered, briefly, if the son he left behind was still alive. He would be big enough to join in the choke-cherry harvest this year.

He shrugged off the thought. Celia was his worry now. She was almost directly below him, where he had reluctantly let her stay put while he crawled up the back rim of the mesa to see who was creeping up on them.

Leaving her there seemed to be Glidinghawk's only option, but he didn't like it. Celia was prone, lying in the meager shade of some cottonwoods, in agony. The quick rise in altitude had temporarily crippled her. It took people that way, sometimes, causing headaches more blinding than lightning.

The mules and horses were out of sight, secured in an arroyo. Glidinghawk had tried to persuade Celia to hide along with them, but she couldn't make it. Tomorrow, if the three of them survived, she should be better. *If* . . . it was a big word.

He saw one of the braves, a silent streak of bronze and buckskin edging toward the cottonwood stand. *I should have dragged Celia out of there by her long red hair,* Glidinghawk thought. *If she was an Indian squaw, I would have. The shady watering hole is the first place they'll look. Now, everything depends on how many of them there are — and how straight I can shoot from this distance.*

The lone brave was like a sitting duck, true, but Glidinghawk hesitated before sighting the Remington. The first Apache, Glidinghawk was sure, was only a decoy.

In a split second, Glidinghawk's suspicion was confirmed. Two more braves appeared in the blink of an eye from around a boulder before once again blending into the dun and rust-colored landscape.

They were moving closer and closer to Celia.

She did not stir. She lay as if dead, with a wet rag turbanning her forehead, covered by the felt, slouch hat that, along with men's breeches, she affected on the trail.

Her stillness, Glidinghawk thought, was good. It might give them both a chance, a few precious minutes, while the Apaches tried to figure out if she was only playing possum. Before leaving her, Glidinghawk had tucked a Peacemaker beside her like a sleeping baby. He hoped she was up to using it.

Glidinghawk watched the scene below him unfold like a tiny illustration in a picture book. He knew he could not count on more time. Once Celia realized the Indians were closing in, once she started firing, the fighting would begin in earnest.

The hairs on the back of Glidinghawk's neck prickled. He breathed in deeply, but it did not steady him.

The dry, hot air scorched his windpipe and his lungs. He raised the rifle.

It glinted in the merciless sun.

He aimed straight down the rim at the lead brave. He cocked the trigger. The rocks behind him dug into his flesh as he tried to stay stock still except for the movement of his arms.

Then he heard it. At first, he thought it was his own clumsiness, a slight shift in footing causing the pebbled scree to shift and skitter.

The skittering sound came again, at first as muted as beads of a rattle in the hands of a waking child, then louder and faster. The sound became a high-pitched warning as irritating as the buzzing of a mosquito.

Glidinghawk tore his gaze way from the drama enfolding below him. His muscles tensed, willing themselves to remain still. Only Gerald's opaque black eyes moved, trying to locate the source of the deadly rattle.

A shriek from below shattered his concentration. His strong, white teeth gritted together, but he did not move.

He saw it now, a sidewinder bellying closer and closer, emerging from the earth like a conqueror. And because it was only a foot long, its venom concentrated in a small package, it was all the more deadly.

A shot echoed from the cold camp. More rifles barked. The sidewinder was aimed in the direction of Glidinghawk's left leg, the one braced in the crevice. Its dry scales undulated in a primitive dance of death.

In the split second it took for Glidinghawk to act, he saw his life unfold before him. He saw the land of his fathers that had once been his. He saw the smiling, pious faces of the Methodist missionaries who had raised him. He saw the cold stone and the colder, stony faces of his fellow students at Dartmouth. He saw the sloe-eyed accusations of the Indian squaw and child he had left behind on the reservation.

Then, these images were replaced by Celia's face, her smiling face when it lit up in laughter, framed by her glowing red hair. Celia was his teammate, an undercover operative like himself—like Landrum Davis, who also respected him. She was also his friend.

Glidinghawk acted.

He shot his left leg out in an arc and whirled furiously out of striking distance as he pivoted around in a backward circle on his right foot. His elbow cracked against the headland rocks, but he did not feel it.

His arms worked in synchronized time. His fingers, which had been grasping the rifle stock, loosened. He tossed the weapon and caught it again. Butt first, he slammed it into the gliding body of the stalking sidewinder. Blood splattered crimson on the already rust-colored rocks.

The snake's head was smashed flat, but its tail sizzled on like a headless warrior, crawling toward the rim and dropping away into nothingness.

Glidinghawk's eyes did not follow its path. He swung the rifle back into firing position and aimed. The Apaches were yelling and crowding in on Celia. Glidinghawk counted four of them—and there were probably more in the hills.

The enemy band knew where he was now. He saw a brave raise a rifle and squeeze off a shot. It whizzed to the right of his head. His ears rang.

He ducked into the cover of rock. Chips of stone flew. He aimed and fired back. He heard a yowl of pain. Maybe he had gotten lucky. He thought he winged one man.

But his position had been announced by the scuffle with the sidewinder. He heard the leather-softened fall of footsteps, the sound of another brave crawling along the ridge. He hoped it was only one man. One man he might be able to kill.

He couldn't tell if the sound was from behind, slightly below or above his toehold on the rim. His heart thudded loudly in his chest as he waited. He needed to know exactly what direction his enemy was coming from.

The plateau and crevice Glidinghawk was holed up in had barely enough room for one man. A mistake would send him spinning out into the void that had taken the sidewinder only moments ago.

There was not enough room to use the Remington at close range. Silently, Glidinghawk tucked it into the slit of the headland and unsheathed his knife. If it were only one man gaining on him, he would have a chance, fighting it out the Indian way. He hoped that Peacemakers—that misnomer for the most popular pistol of the day—were not in this Apache band's armory.

The Apache was good and he was used to the territory. He moved quietly, bounding up rocks and boulders like a born mountain goat. But the brave did not count on Glidinghawk's tenacity and determination.

At the signaling clatter of pebbles—Glidinghawk had loosened them around the perimeter of his vantage point like a protective moat—Glidinghawk sprang from his hiding place.

Arms raised in battle, knife poised like a bird of prey, Glidinghawk let out a loud whoop and holler. The Apache was not expecting it. The brave also had a knife, but Glidinghawk was faster. He slashed downward. His blade bit into muscular flesh, but he failed to cripple the brave's arm that brandished a weapon as finely honed as his own.

The brave slashed out and half stumbled into Glidinghawk, oblivious to pain. Their arms automatically clasped each other, the hands holding the knives straining for action. They were like two beasts mating in a frenzy that would spell death for the weaker one.

The plateau and crevice crowded them together so closely Glidinghawk could smell the bad breath from his opponent's last meal. Glidinghawk felt the sting of the brave's blade slice through the buckskin shirt and dig into his back.

Glidinghawk stilled and garnered his strength. The Apache had felt his blow hit home. He might become confident of victory—so confident he would make a false move.

They were stalemated. The brave snarled in Glidinghawk's face. Glidinghawk started to slash at the Apache. With inhuman effort, he forced himself to stop and wait. They could slash each other into ribbons without either becoming the victor.

From the hidden recesses of Glidinghawk's mind, a channel opened. Instinctively, the moves he had seen Omaha warriors make came back to him. His body remembered the wrestling he had done as a child.

Everything happened in a heartbeat. Glidinghawk didn't know where the messages came from, the signals that coupled boyhood wrestling with the physics he had learned at the university, but they were there like a blessing.

He feigned a slash with his blade. Unexpectedly, he raised his left hand high while snaking a foot around the brave's right knee. Glidinghawk pulled him forward with a hooked ankle. It forced the hinged joint of the brave's knee to buckle inward.

The brave grabbed at Glidinghawk, but Glidinghawk had calculated the angle and the stress. He pulled back, making himself smaller and more solid against the cliff. Glidinghawk ignored his enemy's knife. He willed himself not to feel the second, slicing cut.

Taking the wound worked to his advantage. The momentum arced the brave's spine in the middle, his upper torso thrusting into Glidinghawk while his lower limbs scrabbled fiercely without making purchase. The brave's mouth drew back in a death grimace, a leer of unresigned terror.

Glidinghawk gave one big shove, then used his elbow as a battering ram.

The brave let out a scream that echoed for miles across the barren land. His flailing body dropped for an eternity and landed in a broken heap below, squashed like a summer bug.

Gerald did not waste time.

He secured his blood-stained knife back in his moccasin and grabbed the rifle. He ignored his bleeding wounds. Tending to them would come later.

He surveyed how the fighting was going back in camp as at least four braves moved against a lone woman. But when that woman was Celia there was a chance, Glidinghawk knew. He saw one Apache, gut-shot if his guess was accurate from his distance, not far from where the other brave had landed.

Damn.

Celia must have either run out of ammunition or steam. Glidinghawk saw her now. An Apache was gesturing wildly, his bronzed arms around her slender waist. The brave was pulling the wet cloth and felt slouch hat from her head and pointing at her flaming red hair.

Dear God, not scalping, Glidinghawk thought, praying to the white god before he knew what he was doing. But the warrior was dragging her to his pony as if her entire body was the trophy, not just her scalp.

Apaches liked white women and children as slaves, Glidinghawk knew. Celia had known that, too. She had agreed to this assignment. They had talked about it. But Glidinghawk wondered if she really knew—gut-level—what she was getting into.

Glidinghawk considered taking the chance to pop off a shot, but the brave knew that Celia was his shield as well as his hostage. He had her glued to him closer than flies on stink. There was nothing Gerald could do without the risk of blasting Celia to kingdom come.

He considered killing a few more Apaches just for the hell of it, out of frustration. If Celia hadn't gotten the altitude sickness, if Landrum Davis had won that coin toss and stayed in camp, if that sidewinder hadn't come along at just the wrong moment . . . too many ifs. *Too many ifs.*

The Apaches were gathering together now, far below. They were dragging their corpses along with them. Their dead would be buried before twenty-four hours were up. Otherwise, the Apaches believed, the ghosts of the slain braves would be back to haunt them.

Glidinghawk could give chase and he seriously considered it. But one Indian not used to this land against a band of stirred-up Apaches didn't seem like good odds.

Chances were Davis had heard the shots. Rifle shots carried in this thin air. He was probably headed back to camp now, cautiously. Glidinghawk hated to have to give him the news of Celia's capture.

But maybe together the two of them could track the Chiricahua and break Celia free before—

Before things that Glidinghawk didn't want to think about.

Right now, there were a few points Glidinghawk had to hold onto. First, the Apaches probably thought he was dead. They could very well believe that the brave in the headlands had killed him.

Moreover, the band didn't know about Landrum Davis.

Last, the raiders had been too excited about their red-headed captive to track down the pack mules and horses, at least so far.

But somehow, all that didn't make Gerald Glidinghawk feel a helluva lot better. He had killed several Apaches. He felt responsible for Celia's capture. And this mission had him spooked deep inside in a way he couldn't explain to anyone, red or white.

He almost wished it had been him, tumbling off the cliff into nothingness. He tried to make his mind a blank, but he had used up his ration of will power for the day.

Instead, he remembered his uneasy feelings that this

mission had been jinxed from the start. He remembered how they had all ended up here, risking their lives for a Lt. Col. Amos Powell and the U.S. Army.

CHAPTER TWO

They had outfitted at the Southwest Territorial Command north of Tucson, assembling pack mules and ponies, canteens and leather water pouches, dried rations. They had also sewn gold into the linings of their saddlebags. For their cover as slavers, they would require hard cash.

They needed beasts that could weather the bleached-bone climate and keep a steady footing where canyons, mesas and rims fell away in vertical drops, zigzagging through the Arizona Territory like the prominent vertebrae of an arched buffalo hump. The hump jutted up from the body of desert hardpan in a crooked northwest to southeast line.

They were Powell's Army, a moniker some wag in Washington City had jokingly bestowed on them. There were only three of them. And since one was a woman and another an Indian, in many white men's pale eyes that left only an army of one. Lt. Col. Amos Powell didn't see the humor.

Humor was also in short supply in the Arizona Territory in July. The heat was brutal — over 100 in the shade — and the dryness sucked the moisture from their skin, making the membranes of their mouths and noses as dry and raspy as unginned cotton.

Celia had already decided that ladies out here sweat. Perspire was too genteel a word and she told Davis and Glidinghawk as much. The sweat evaporated before it made rings under their armpits, leaving a salty film on their skin.

Like Celia, Glidinghawk was used to more temperate weather. A fine, powdery dust overlay his bronzed limbs.

It was bad enough now on the northern rim of the plateau Tucson sprang from to lure men from nearby Fort Lowell—tough men—who found desertion a good alternative to desert madness. The garrison was stuck up north of the city, isolated and barren unless you had a fondness for rattlers, lizards, and cacti.

The fort was adobe, Mex construction, and that had helped some. Out in the wilderness, up through the gorges and into the Gila Mountains, or south into the Sonoran desert that extended into Mexico, it would be worse.

All three had dreaded it. Their minds floated like hawks on an updraft in the oxygen-poor altitude, soaring between the exultation of tracking their prey and their awesome respect for the harsh distances.

It was about like being plunked down off the edge of the known world, they decided. A man or woman out here felt about as small as a grain of sand, dwarfed by the primitive vastness. Earth, Fire, Wind and Sky, even a born and bred Methodist felt the power of the Indian gods.

And their mission was only beginning.

They had received their orders after the Fort Griffin

affair, their first mission together. They had cleaned up The Flats—notorious pigpens in a land not known for couth—and caught a cold-blooded killer. They had faced death together and won.

They had drawn closer, as Amos Powell had hoped they would. Still, they were an unusual trio. Landrum Davis, 41, was honed by the battles of his life and he still had a minie ball in the ass to prove it. He boasted about it.

Code name, Operative C.

A former Confederate officer and Texas Ranger, Davis was taciturn but shrewd. Piercing eyes, hawk nose, saber scar across his lean and hungry face, he was a skilled hunter and outdoorsman. And yet Davis was so quiet sometimes it was hard to recognize his strength—until you came up against it.

Celia Louise Burnett, 21, code name Operative A, was a whole new bailiwick. Sure, Pinkerton was using some female operatives these days, but they were few and far between. And none of them could top Celia for looks or sheer spunk.

Maybe Celia had to be tough, under all that honey, being the daughter of an army officer killed in the Oregon Trail Massacre. Maybe that aunt of hers up in Massachusetts got Celia's back up, sending her to Miss Parsons Finishing School and trying to make a proper lady out of her.

Anyway, Celia was gorgeous, with her flaming red hair and emerald green eyes, but she could also deal cards, handle small weapons and calm the fury of a spooked mustang. Celia had proved herself back in Texas. As Landrum said, when there weren't any females in earshot, she wasn't cherry anymore. She was better. He wasn't talking about her womanhood, either, though he knew about her affair with that gambler back in Griffin.

Gerald Glidinghawk was the third member of Powell's Army. Operative B. 23 years old. A Dartmouth-educated Omaha who couldn't make it in the Indian world any more than he could the white man's world. He was a chameleon, fitting in where he needed to.

Generally speaking, he showed about as much emotion as the carved idol he resembled, but both Celia and Davis had found something warm and honest about him. He was unusual for a man of any color.

None of them fit in just where they were supposed to. That's probably why Lieutenant Colonel Powell, from the U.S. Army Territorial Command up in Fort Leavenworth, Kansas, had chosen them.

Powell had a feeling that only smart oddballs, working undercover, could clean up certain messes, like whiskey trade to the tribes and control of businesses of ill-repute and so on. Amos had been right, too, judging from Fort Griffin.

There was a fourth member of the team, but he was spit and polish, military. Preston Kirkwood Fox, 21, straight out of West Point. In these dealings, that was no recommendation. Still, he was official liaison between the team and the army, though Amos would like to change that.

Fox had almost gotten them all killed with his hidebound belief that the military rulebook came first, but he had come through. There might be hope for the pompous second lieutenant yet. He would be up at Fort Apache, acting as an officer. Maybe this time, he would be smarter, more suspicious of the other military men than he was of A, B and C.

Together, they had survived their first case.

This one would be tougher.

First, they were starting out in the heat of summer in a hostile land. Then came the complications of being caught in the middle between the suspects up at Fort Apache — at least two regular army men and maybe more — and the Apaches, particularly the Chiricahua. Old Cochise, the latrine rumors had it, was savagely unhappy about those missing Indian maidens.

The commander of Fort Lowell, a lieutenant colonel named Smith, was supposed to be on their side. He needed their help even if it was hard for him to swallow, a trifle unorthodox for his tastes. But Smith was willing to try anything if it would quell the Apache uprisings.

Fort Lowell was a couple of hundred miles south of Fort Apache and not as much of a wilderness outpost, though it sure seemed like it after five days of relentless sun.

Powell's team needed the mules, the horses, the hard cash from the army, but when it came right down to it, none of them felt safe connecting up with the garrison in broad daylight. Gossip spread.

And then, from what Powell had written, those Mexican slavers were as fierce as any bandeleros along the border. Celia had been downright relieved to ditch her Fort Griffin cover as a faro dealer, until these new orders came through. This case could make the skulduggery at The Flats look like a Sunday school picnic. If they survived it.

Davis and Glidinghawk had both blanched about the same color when they read Amos Powell's orders. Ghost white without a hint of tan or bronze. Celia, who didn't know the terrain, was a little more sanguine, until they started heading due west from Texas through the Panhandle.

Their orders had read:

To A, B, C,
From AP

You are directed to proceed to the vicinity of Fort Apache, Arizona Territory. We have reason to believe a certain Captain Honorius Crawford is nefariously engaged in kidnapping and selling young Apache maidens to Mexican slavers for carnal or domestic purposes. We believe a certain Master Sergeant Joseph Tibbs is involved along with a ring of enlisted men. We have no certain evidence, but Crawford and Tibbs appear to have more money than army pay could account for. Seventeen Apache women are known to be missing.

You are to set yourselves up as slavers and attempt to trap the miscreants. Crawford and Tibbs are experts at arms and extremely dangerous. You will be equally in peril from rival Mexican slavers. If you should get into trouble south of the border, there is no way we can help you.

The disappearance of the Apache maidens and rumors of their maltreatment in Mexico are causing great unrest among those Apache bands, including the Chiricahua, who are least reconciled to reservation life, and could lead to new outbreaks in the continuing Apache wars.

"There's more here than Powell is telling us," Landrum had said. "What do you make of it, Gerald?"

"He either thinks Texas was too soft for us, he hates us, or the situation is about to blow up. Something like this is all Cochise needs to get all the tribes behind him. And he's enough of a threat as it is. Arizona Territory in July isn't exactly a choice spot."

"I've never been to Arizona," Celia offered. "Could it be worse than summer in Texas?" She sounded eager, but the taut faces of the two men gave her pause.

"It's hotter than Hades," Landrum told her. He tried to grin. He liked Celia. He was glad to see her coming back to life. The last assignment had been especially tough on her. It hadn't made her quit, though.

Glidinghawk squinted into the sun, as if peering into the future. He spoke carefully. "Out there, the greatest enemy we have is the land, and all the others go along with it. If we take too long to act, there's a chance the kidnappings will bring the different Apache tribes together in a common cause. That will get Indians wiped out as well as white men—and there aren't too many of us redskins left."

Glidinghawk's voice trailed off. Davis knew what the Indian was thinking. Most of his people had been killed or starved off. He was a survivor. He wanted his people to survive. And his people were no longer the isolated band of Omahas he had been born into, but all Indians.

Glidinghawk knew that fighting the white man would not work. Ultimately, they could only endure, bend like reeds in the wind. Dartmouth had given him an unusual point of view for an Indian, one Davis respected.

"So what plan would you recommend?" Davis asked. As senior operative, Davis could have made the decisions and given the orders. It was a mark of the man that, in this situation, he deferred to Gerald. His attitude was uncommon in a land where a white man was brought up to see all redskins as primitive savages.

"Get going as soon as possible. Make the break from the military at another garrison far from Fort Apache. We need to make contact with both the Chiricahuas and the Mexican slavers as a team, totally separate from the army."

Landrum nodded. He added only one comment. "Danged if I look forward to a sorry-assed stage ride. But it's the quickest way."

And it was. The grinding, teeth-chattering, kidney-jarring Butterfield Stage scrabbled day and night through the flat hardpans and up, always up, to the mesas and canyons and headlands. "I'll kiss the ground Fort Lowell stands on," Celia said, "as long as it doesn't bounce."

But the overland stage was only a foretaste of what was to come. Bedding down on the cornhusk mattresses of the outpost while they made preparations for the desert wilderness was the easy part.

Actually, only Celia and Landrum Davis bedded down on the mattresses in segregated quarters, with Celia well chaperoned, courtesy of Lt. Col. Smith and his raw-boned, parched-skinned wife. They were given access to the officers' single, private outhouses.

Gerald Glidinghawk, though part of the team, bedded down in the stable. Other Indians employed by the army congregated there. Injuns were said to be good with horses.

Glidinghawk would have scorned the enlisted men's bunks and fourholer, even if they had been offered. He preferred mules and horses to a herd of hardcase soldiers. Like the Indian scouts who worked for the fort, he voided in the desert in privacy, and covered his leavings with earth. It was the Indian way.

Celia found him, coming back to the garrison, in the late afternoon shortly before their departure from the fort. Landrum was in conference with Smith. She had not been included. Neither had Gerald.

She raised her arm in greeting. A garrison soldier on watch about 20 yards behind her—the one who sucked on his bad teeth and warned her about going off post—spat on the ground. The soldier hawked so loud the sound carried. Glidinghawk heard it, as he was intended to. His face froze in midsmile.

"Women and Indians are kept in their place around here," Celia commented briefly. "I don't believe they trust us. I'm immoral and you're shifty."

"I thought the ladies were giving you a tea," Gerald said.

"They did, along with sermons. I escaped," Celia admitted. "I don't know how my mother could stand it, God rest her soul. Officers' wives are starved for outside company, even for the likes of me, but the main idea was to keep me occupied so the commander could talk to Landrum without my interference."

They strolled at an angle to the fort, away from the daytime sentry's post. Their footsteps kicked up whorls of dust. Gerald lowered his voice. Mockingly, he spoke the way an Indian was expected to, in pidgin.

"Indians say Smith is fair man. No like women, except to cook. Maybe good for bedtime games. No like Indians, but is fair man. Lieutenant Colonel is heap big worried. Scouts see war paint and war bonnets, many braves, on Yoche Ha-hao-pi trail. Big talk granddaughter of Cochise is taken."

"Then we're too late?" Celia asked.

Gerald whirled around in a complete circle like a dervish. Satisfied that no one was within the sound of their voices — and that the fort guard had resumed his bored, somnolent stare — he dropped his pidgin and his stiff, wooden Indian stare.

"This is all rumor so far. Davis is probably being briefed now. It doesn't look good, but there hasn't been an Apache war council yet. The granddaughter's name is Saguaro Flower. They say she is the old chief's favorite, and the old man is dying. He wants her back before he dies. She could have been taken by a rival tribe, but personally, I doubt it."

"Does this make a big difference to us?"

"It makes the Chiricahua Apaches angrier, and most of them were born angry. Apaches are the most feared Indians around here, but the different tribes mistrust each other. About the only thing they agree on is the Paiutes, who are from a different family altogether. Paiutes capture slaves too.

"A lot depends on whether the Chiricahua make the connection between the white soldiers and the missing girl. Could be some Apache and Paiutes end up killing each other.

"The army would probably like that. But if Cochise's band finds it was soldiers responsible, the forts could be attacked."

Celia's brilliant eyes clouded. "For you, there's no way to win, is there?"

Glidinghawk surprised her. He grinned. "Maybe some devious maneuvering will work. I don't want to see either an Indian bloodbath or a white massacre. But it would not break my heart to see these Mexican slavers slaughtered. And I have a lead on the worst of them."

"Is this what Landrum is learning right now?"

"No, I don't believe so. This came from one of the scouts, who was trying to buy himself a squaw. It isn't the kind of information you pass on to an army man who doesn't exactly cotton to depraved, amoral Indians. This scout mentioned a slaver by the name of Sexto Diaz, who has a camp up in the Gilas and sells slaves out of Sonora."

"You mean Mexico?"

"*Si, senorita*. I have a hunch we are in for some foreign travel. But first, I think we'd better get you back to the garrison. By now, we probably have all the tongues wagging, consorting this way."

Celia looked around. The sharp, blue-black shadows had deepened, slicing like knives across the bleak landscape. Lights were coming on in the garrison.

And, Celia recalled, she had promised Davis she would comport herself as a lady, at least until they got out of here. Ladies did not go off bounds or engage in conversations with Indians.

As she separated from Glidinghawk — the Indian heading in the direction of the stables with only a curt nod of farewell — Celia looked out at the overwhelming expanse of burnt sienna slashed with purple black. A tremor ran through her, a mixture of anticipation and fear.

Glidinghawk slipped his Indian mask back over his face. His high cheekbones and strongly etched nose, his Mongolian eyes as black as anthracite coal, made him look as noble and distant as the bust on a coin. He walked on silent, moccasined feet. He, too, shivered.

Glidinghawk felt the deadly pull of the earth drawing him like a magnet. He felt the threat and power calling him out there. He thought he had left the superstition of shamanism behind, but the first hoot of the night owl, the Death Owl, pierced him like an arrow.

It was not only for himself that he felt fear. At that moment, he felt not as a single man, but as part of the brotherhood of men, both red and white. He walked more quickly, head bowed.

For the first time since he had signed up with Lt. Col. Amos Powell, Glidinghawk began to feel he had a personal stake in this mission beyond earning the $66.67 a month pay that had been promised to him.

It was a disquieting feeling.

He hoped the second, triumphant shriek of the Death Owl was not an omen.

CHAPTER THREE

The Death Owl.

Glidinghawk shed the thought like a snake sheds its old skin, with difficulty. What he heard in his ears now was only a ringing, the after-effect of the rifles blasting and echoing through the gorge. Besides, he had work to do.

If the Chiricahua came back, Glidinghawk knew their first interest would be the livestock. There was nothing a Chiricahua liked more than fresh roasted horse, unless it was fresh roasted pack mule. They preferred horsemeat and mule flesh to buffalo, deer or antelope. Captured animals were run to the ground, then eaten.

The first thing Glidinghawk did, even before tending to his wounds, was creep down the arroyo and check on the animals. In the back of Gerald's mind, something was working on him, something odd. Raiding livestock usually came first with the Chiricahua, before taking captives.

But the Indian band had not discovered the beasts

or, at least, had not taken the time to capture them. Glidinghawk's spirits rose a little when he saw them, and then sank when he saw an arrow had pierced the biggest water pouch, the one carried by the dun colored mule Celia had named Hope.

So one of the braves had located the animals after all. Glidinghawk hoped the Indian had met his death before he reported the location. Otherwise, the raiders would be back.

The mules, Faith and Charity, were all right, as were their loads. Celia's horse, an appaloosa she insisted on calling Surefoot in the hope the name would rub off, looked frightened, but Glidinghawk's small gelding was calm. He nickered at his owner's approach.

"Steady, boy," Glidinghawk said, stroking the horse's velvety muzzle. He freed the gelding first, then the placid mules, and last the quivering appaloosa. He gathered them around him and took them into a sliver of shade cast by the dry-rocked depression.

Glidinghawk looked at the sun, now well past its zenith, and decided to stay in the shelter of the gully until it sank further in the sky, or until he heard Landrum Davis approach. He knew that the Chiricahua were afraid of the spirits that roamed the night.

While he waited, Glidinghawk stripped the buckskin shirt from his torso and washed his knife cuts with water from the leaking water pouch. The gash on his back, along his lower rib cage, gave him the most trouble. He packed it with a poultice of herbs, wincing at the sting.

The other cut — the one that saved his life by throwing the enemy brave off balance — had only grazed nerves and skin without butchering flesh. Overall,

Glidinghawk felt fortunate his injuries were not worse.

He was weak, though. He took a long draw of water and forced himself to chew some beef jerky. He waited. The purple haze of twilight was coloring the sky by the time he heard shod horsehooves circling around.

Landrum, Glidinghawk hoped.

He took a chance, but not before mounting his horse and readying his Remington. "Is it you, the hider from Fort Griffin?" he shouted.

Strange, that Indian superstitions were crowding Glidinghawk. He couldn't bear to shout out Landrum's name, in case their enemies were nearby.

"That you, Glidinghawk?" Davis boomed. Glidinghawk tightened. He didn't want foes to hear his own name, either.

"It sure as hell isn't an Apache," Glidinghawk yelled back. "I'm coming up to the camp. Wait for me."

Davis was waiting with his firearm out and cocked, until he saw Glidinghawk was indeed alone. Gerald tethered the beasts to a cottonwood, motioned to Davis, and squatted on the ground. The Indian's face was lined and haggard.

As they settled themselves, Landrum began, "I heard rifles and headed back, but I had gone further than I thought. Made better speed with only one horse, or I never would have made it by dark . . ."

Davis paused, staring down at the ground in front of his feet. He did not want to ask about Celia. He had had a bad feeling this morning, leaving camp. Now, it ached like a blow in the gut.

"Apaches. Chiricahua. Maybe a half dozen. I killed at least one, and Celia shot one. I might have been able to pick them off from up there," Gerald motioned to the headland above them, "but a damned rattler came along. I don't understand why the braves didn't track our animals, but they took off with Celia instead, before they got around to it. They headed west. Maybe we can catch up with them."

"What do you figure they'll do with her?" Landrum asked, his strong, deep voice shaky.

"Make her a slave, if she's lucky. Didn't look like they were going to scalp her. Not on the spot, anyway."

"Do you think we stand a chance of getting her back?" Davis asked. A silence as quiet as despair followed his words.

Glidinghawk answered slowly, choosing his words with care. He had spent all afternoon thinking about it, about what he knew of the Chiricahua and their customs in this strange, overwhelming land.

He told Davis some of what he knew of Apache superstitions and how they might be used against the raiding band who had captured Celia. Wisely, Glidinghawk did not mention the primitive fears and superstitions that had come back to haunt him. They had enough problems to deal with, without that.

"Going fishing!" Landrum exploded. "Are you trying to play some kind of joke on me?"

"No," Gerald said, quite sincere. Davis studied the Indian's somber face. Glidinghawk was just as upset about Celia as he was. "One thing that the Chiricahua are deathly afraid of is fish. There's a river. Further down, a shallow mudhole. I'm going to go catch us some fish. I suggest you make us some coffee. We need to get Celia before sun-up, so it will be a very long night."

Davis built a quick fire and threw coffee grounds into the chipped enameled pot. Cowboy style coffee would put some starch in their spines tonight. He craved a hot, bitter cup right now, but the time it took to make a small fire and coffee seemed to stretch on and on.

The fire, at this point, would make no difference. They would be long gone before daylight. But damned if the felt like making a comfortable camp while the Chiricahua were doing God-knows-what to Celia.

Time was another enemy, tonight. They had until daylight to find the Chiricahua band and make their best stand. In daylight, they wouldn't have a chance.

Davis' curiosity finally got the better of him. He had to see what Glidinghawk was up to. Fish? He could not believe that fish could even exist out here. Glidinghawk, though, insisted that there might be shad or perhaps carp.

Once the coffeepot was bubbling, Davis ambled down to where he heard splashing. The mudhole spilled over in a saucer depression, fanning out from the main trickle of current. It was flat and muddy, with algae scummed at the edges. Glidinghawk's clothes were lying on the bank.

"They're here all right," Glidinghawk said. "Fast little buggers." He lunged headfirst, arms flailing at the water, and came up with a wet face and empty hands. In the twilight, his buttocks cleared the waterline and winked wetly at Davis. He dove back underwater.

In spite of everything, Landrum laughed. He roared. Glidinghawk surfaced spluttering, again empty-handed.

"Don't you know grappling, boy?" Landrum bellowed.

Davis shed his clothes and waded in. He saw the flash of the now agitated fish, bumping and darting and skipping the waterline. They had never been exposed to men before. These clumsy creatures were greatly disturbing their tranquility.

Slipping on a mud-slick, Davis ended on his ass. The water was hot, but cooler than the surrounding air. It reminded him of swimming in cattle tanks when he was a boy. He splashed muddy water over his face. His skin turned muck-colored, like Glidinghawk's. The two men stared at each other. Under other circumstances, it might have been fun.

"I can tell you weren't brought up in Texas," Landrum said. "First, you have to have a plan. Scare the fish into a shallow. Then one of us has to grab quicker than lightning striking. Here. You splash them over there, to that corner of the hole, and I'll wait. They try to swim away, you splash like hell and they'll jump around right into my waiting arms. Works every time."

Half an hour and 20 grabs later, Davis pulled his first fish, wriggling and slimy, out of the mudhole. They both cheered. The fish gasped its last in Landrum's talon-like grip.

For good measure, they caught two more. It went quicker, as the two men got their system down. At three fish, Glidinghawk said, "Enough. We'd better get going — and pray this works."

The Chiricahua's trail was not too difficult to follow, especially since they had been forewarned that the renegade band had reverted to their former, pre-reservation ways.

Before they had left Fort Lowell, one of the Indian stablehands told Glidinghawk that the rebel Indians used to camp between the Black River and the San Francisco fork of the Gila, in the foothills, when summer came.

Although the Chiricahua were nomadic, there was a pattern to their seasonal migrations, before the white man came along and decreed otherwise. When Davis and Glidinghawk lost track of the raiding band several times, Glidinghawk had guessed that the instinct of centuries had prevailed.

Then, too, the stablehand, himself an Apache from a tribe rival to the Chiricahua, had drawn Glidinghawk a crude map in the dirt. As it turned out, his information was vital.

Several miles into the desert, Davis was certain that the three shad in his saddlebags had lost their silvery-black sheen and fresh-eyed stare.

Davis and Glidinghawk stopped about three miles south of where they estimated the Chiricahua to be. There, Glidinghawk began tying circles of buckskin around their horses' feet with strips of rawhide. They had ridden hard through jagged hills and desert hardpan, after leaving their spot by Gila San Francisco. A full moon was out.

"First dead fish, now horse booties," Davis observed, incredulous. "I hope to hell you know what you're doing. What we are doing," he amended. "What *are* we doing?"

"You'll see," Glidinghawk grinned.

Davis snorted. There was a lot he wanted to see. Preparing to go up against the Chiricahua was the damnedest experience he'd ever been through.

But he trusted Glidinghawk. Davis knew that the Indian's unusual mind was the best weapon they had against the hostile Chiricahua band.

"They do look like booties," Glidinghawk agreed, surveying the horses' softly shod forelegs. "Nothing alerts an Indian more than the sound of horseshoe iron. That metal hitting a hard surface means soldiers to them, and this band is probably on the lookout for men from Fort Apache. I would guess they are a good fifty miles south of their reservation."

As they continued into the three mile perimeter of the Chiricahua summer camp, Davis and Glidinghawk knew they would have to exercise extreme caution. They could expect outer guards in another two miles, or a mile out of the settlement. These would be their first challenge. Further in, there would be more guards.

Two men breaking in on an Apache band in the middle of the night without getting killed or captured seemed pretty near impossible to Davis. If it were anyone but Celia in there, he would have walked away.

Glidinghawk, too, had his doubts.

But it *was* Celia in there.

So they would try, armed with the best weapons the U.S. Army had come up with for them. Their guns weren't standard army issue, since they were undercover operatives, but a damned sight more sophisticated than the bows and arrows and single action Charlesville .69 muskets the Apache were sure to have.

But the Remingtons and Peacemakers and razor-sharp knives were nothing, Glidinghawk insisted, compared to the cunning they would need.

Davis nodded. It was not a yes or no nod. It was a

puzzled nod. "I don't know about this," he finally said, "I've never gone up against an enemy armed with a small mess of dead fish."

CHAPTER FOUR

"Why they would want to make summer camp out here is beyond me," Davis said, shaking his head.

Glidinghawk finished with Surefoot's forelegs and straightened. His own gelding, which he had refused to name, and Davis' large sorrel Devil, were already booted.

"If the Fort Apache Reservation is like most, it probably makes this look like a garden paradise," Glidinghawk said. "Are we ready?"

"As ready as we'll ever be," Landrum replied, wrinkling his nose at the fish stench from his saddlebag.

They cantered for the next mile, halted to check the booties, and walked the beasts for the penultimate mile. Just short of the one mile perimeter from the Chiricahua camp—if their guess about its location was right—they dismounted.

For the first phase of their plan, Davis would wait with the tethered horses, and those stinking fish, while Glidinghawk proceeded on foot.

They had agreed that they wanted all three horses as close to the enemy camp as they dared bring them. If they managed to free Celia, they wanted to be able to ride away fast and furiously.

The pack mules were tied to a boulder several miles away, yet further back along their proposed escape route.

If Glidinghawk and Davis did not survive, neither would the animals. Several days in the scorching sun without water and the mules would die from dehydration, too weak to free themselves.

The horses, being close to the invisible border the renegade band patrolled, would be discovered before they died of thirst. They would become a Chiricahuan feast.

Davis and Glidinghawk hated to leave any of the animals vulnerable, but there was no better alternative.

"If I don't return by sunrise, ride like hell out of here," Glidinghawk told Davis. "Due east would be good. Save yourself, because there will be nothing you can do for Celia . . . or for me."

"You'll make it," Landrum said. "You'd better. I don't want to be cheated out of scaring the living bejesus out of this slave-happy band."

Glidinghawk smiled, but his lips were drawn thin. He needed the element of surprise on his side. That, and the Apaches' fear of the night, were his only hope. But the Apache were changing, adapting to the ways of white men. Darkness could no longer be counted on to keep them from fighting at night.

The two men shook hands solemnly, each knowing that he might be seeing the other for the last time.

"Take care," Landrum whispered gruffly.

The Indian slipped away.

Glidinghawk padded softly forward with the litheness and stealth of a cougar. His narrowed eyes surveyed the terrain. Beyond the depression where he had left Davis with the horses was a slight rise leading up a needletop outcropping of rock.

There was too much guesswork, too many ifs. But if Glidinghawk's gut feeling was correct, a Chiricahua scout was manning that stone turret.

The way Apaches guarded their camps, Glidinghawk knew, was with a double ring of guards. At the outer level, about at the one-mile distance from camp, there were generally three guards, posted like the points on a triangle.

Three braves would be waiting at these points, the spots with the highest elevation, with miles of empty territory between them.

The way Gerald figured it, the brave he had to take out would be right up there on the needletop, waiting, watching.

If he could kill that one, he and Landrum would be able to sneak in on the second, more heavily manned ring of guards.

Glidinghawk wiped that clean from his mind. First things first.

The moon had been a blessing earlier. Now it was a curse. Glidinghawk eased himself into a crouch and made about 100 yards before falling flat on his belly.

He had left both his pistol and rifle behind. Unless he could take this guard out in man-to-man combat, his plan would never work. He needed a silent kill.

Being armed only with his knife made it easier for Glidinghawk to slither the last yards to the base of the rock formation. So far, so good.

Gerald concentrated on his own movements, on the silent victory of every inch of ground he covered. Deep inside, he knew he was about to kill a man, an Indian like himself. He knew that the brave waiting up there had a family, a mother, a father, a grandfather, maybe even children of his own.

But white men against red men, Indians against their brothers, these were the times he lived in, Glidinghawk thought.

And maybe, if Glidinghawk succeeded in killing this lone Indian, and went on to accomplish this small mission, maybe not so many men would have to die.

Or was Glidinghawk only justifying the battle fever coursing through him, demanding victory? The adrenaline lifted him up to a plane of vitality different from everyday life, with its small and measured rhythms.

Time stood still. There was only that further inch up the rock, the deadly knife, the muscles tensed for survival.

The way the rocks had formed in primordial times, there was a slight incline, then a whopping tower jutting almost vertically upward to the sky.

And on the very top, Glidinghawk saw the figure of a man, saw him silhouetted like a sentry of the gods. The brave was still and quiet, but whether it was because he had heard or suspected nothing, or because he sensed danger nearby the way an animal sometimes does, Glidinghawk could not tell.

There were toeholds in the steep rock tower, a natural stairway that had been used for hundreds of years. The edges of the stairs were worn smooth. Glidinghawk climbed slowly, thinking it was all too convenient, too easy. He knew that at least one step along the way would contain a secret danger.

The needletop was perhaps 20 feet high, small enough to be dwarfed by a mountain, but tall enough to make the surrounding earth seem flat and lacking in majesty. Glidinghawk had climbed up to almost 15 feet.

His eyes scanned ahead. He felt, rather than saw, the trap just above him. He knew it had to be there, where the smooth stone put in place by man rather than nature beckoned invitingly.

Glidinghawk could not see it well, so he ran his fingertips over it, feeling how it was slightly different from the natural stone steps. He felt to the left. Rock wall and nothing else. To the right there was tricky outcropping of jagged rock that looked deceptively fragile.

Glidinghawk stopped. He closed his eyes, fingertips still connecting with what appeared to be the next stair up, his other hand barely touching the rough rock.

Like a telegraph current, a message came through clearly to him. The way that appeared safer meant death. The difficult way, scrambling to the right, clutching the jagged handholds and swinging his full weight over the drop, connected only by a jagged piece of stone, would give him a chance at life.

These feelings were so strong Glidinghawk did not hesitate. The earth had talked to him, giving up her secrets. He trusted the force he felt.

He placed his foot confidently on the small patch of stone to his right. His hands clutched the minute hold above for balance. His body swung out in an arc. Nothing was beneath him but air and the niche that held his foot. It held fast.

He pulled himself another foot up and swung back in toward the stairway. For the moment, he was safe. He stopped and breathed deeply. He would have to come down the same way.

Glidinghawk took his time, crawling only a fraction of an inch at a time. The slowness was agonizing, but it was the only way. So far, the sentry was not aware of his presence.

His head was almost level with the top of the formation. Strangely, the moon cast the shadow of Glidinghawk's enemy directly on him. From that shadow, he could see that the brave was turned away from him.

This time, there could be no yelling.

Out there, listening, were many more braves.

This time, there could be no struggle or chance.

Glidinghawk pulled the knife from his moccasin. He cradled it in his hand. He held the sharp edge outward, ready for action.

He saw the Chiricahua's head turn.

Glidinghawk pressed his face against the hard rock. He willed himself to become solid as stone. The brave belched once and walked over to the dizzying 20 foot drop. He stared straight out. He laid his toughened leather shield and lance down beside him.

Using both his hands, the brave reached for his crotch and proceeded to relieve himself over the side, aiming his stream of urine in the direction of the wind.

Glidinghawk knew he would never have a better chance.

He leapt straight up over the top of the rim. He rammed right into the sentry's back. His left arm grasped the brave's torso around the waist. His right arm swung the knife into action.

Glidinghawk's blade sliced through the man's throat just as he started to scream. Only a bloody gurgle erupted. The brave's hands loosened their hold on his genitals.

The Apache's entire body convulsed. His hands dropped, twitching, to his side. His throat was slashed from ear to ear.

Crimson spurted everywhere from arterial wounds. Glidinghawk's hands and knife were slick with blood. The Apache was very dead.

Gently, Glidinghawk lowered the brave to the needletop, to his final resting place. He closed the dead Indian's eyes, and arranged his arms and legs in a pose of peace.

Ceremoniously, Glidinghawk placed five canted rocks on top of the Chiricahua's corpse. It was not much of a burial, but it was the best he could do.

Closing his own dark, Indian-slanted eyes, Glidinghawk tried to think of a prayer. But none would come to him, not from the Christian God, not from the Indian gods.

Finally, he said the only words of comfort he could think of. "Peace, brother," Glidinghawk murmured into the night wind that was kicking up. "Peace."

The trip down the needletop proved more of a

challenge. Glidinghawk had the sentry's lance and shield to carry, as well as the dead man's buckskin breechcloth.

The single leather thong that had held the Chiricahua's long, straight hair back away from his head, Glidinghawk had tied around his own head of black hair.

When he descended to the 15 foot level, Glidinghawk looked at the trap step. His curiosity got the better of him. From above, he prodded the suspect stair with his foot. It toppled loose and crashed down to the bottom of the rock formation.

Again, Glidinghawk used the jagged foothold, zigzagging out into space before securing his footing again. It was tougher to maneuver, going down, but he made it. His confidence was coming back to him.

He was on the slight incline, almost back to terra firma, when he stopped dead in his tracks. Protectively, he raised the Apache shield in front of him.

"Hey! It's me," Landrum called.

It was moments before Glidinghawk could speak. When he was able, his fear turned to anger. "What the hell are you doing here?" he demanded. "You are supposed to be back with the horses ready to save your own ass. For all you knew, I could be a scalping Indian coming after you."

"Don't get your balls in an uproar," Landrum said, grinning wildly. "If you were, I about decided it was a damned sight better than waiting it out alone with those stinking fish."

"You're the one who keeps talking about orders and planning," Glidinghawk snapped. "What made you change your mind?"

"I didn't want any Indian playing hero without giving me a chance to join in," Landrum shot back. "I began to figure that if you were killed, I was going to try to get Celia out by myself. And if you weren't, it would be faster if you didn't have to go back to get me. And for the record, I'm damned glad you are still alive."

Glidinghawk's expression was not easy to read. He started to say something, but the words broke deep in his chest. He gave up and silently held up the prizes he had taken from the Chiricahua sentry.

Davis examined them.

He looked his Omaha friend over.

Without speaking, Glidinghawk shed his buffalo-skin shirt and trousers. He stripped himself of the white man's underwear he had grown used to wearing. For an instant, he thought of what the missionaries who raised him would say to this scene. He remembered boyhood battles about underwear and its proper place in the scheme of life.

Gerald . . . the name hardly fitted him when he tied the brief breechcloth around his waist. It covered his loins, and little else. Glidinghawk shouldered the lance and shield and scowled fiercely. He looked like a Chiricahua warrior, even at this close distance.

"You are a danged genius," Landrum finally said. "If you had been in the war on the Confederate side, I bet we would have won."

Glidinghawk understood what Davis was trying to say, in his rough way. Landrum rarely spoke of the Civil War or the beating he had taken, fighting for the southern cause. It did not matter. In his own way, Davis was giving Glidinghawk the highest compliment he could think of.

"Who cares about old wars?" Glidinghawk asked, his voice working almost normally. "We have a helluva battle coming up. At least now, I think the odds have turned in our favor."

"I believe you are right," Landrum agreed. Then he added, "And I'm damned glad you are on my side on this one. Just tell me what to do next, and I'll see if I can improve on taking orders."

CHAPTER FIVE

With the disguise, taking out the second guard was easier. Glidinghawk walked to within six feet of him before the Chiricahua brave's eyes widened in terror. By then, it was too late. Glidinghawk's lance had pierced the man's jugular, its sharp metal point coming out cleanly from the other side of the neck.

Modern times, Glidinghawk thought. The lance was a primitive weapon compared to the repeating rifles and six-shooters of the white men, but the Apaches now tipped those, and their arrows, with the white man's cast-off metal. It updated them.

The guard who formed the third point of the protective triangle was on the other side of the Indian camp. Glidinghawk decided that they should not worry about him — until later, anyway.

As it was, time was growing short; they had only a few hours left until sunrise.

By now, Landrum and Glidinghawk worked as a well-rehearsed team. Landrum had gone back for the horses. The value of their buckskin booties was even more apparent. When the animals walked, their hoofbeats made no more noise than a quiet man's footsteps.

"We'll let Surefoot carry this dead guard until we can see the wickiups," Glidinghawk decided. "Once those are in sight, I want you to tether our mounts so they can be untied quickly. I'll drag the body from there."

"Right," Landrum grunted, heaving the Indian's body up and tying it over the saddle.

"What are you doing?" Glidinghawk asked sharply.

Without asking, Landrum was shedding his own clothing and dressing in the second guard's Apache garb. They had been fortunate, just plain lucky. This brave had a Charlesville .69 hidden behind his shield — and he hadn't gotten a chance to use it.

Glidinghawk could not keep his lips from twitching when he saw Landrum Davis all decked out.

"You'd never make a heathen," Glidinghawk said. "Legs like that could only belong to a white man."

And it was true. Although Landrum's hair was dark enough to pass in the night — at a distance — and the skin of his face and hands was deeply tanned, almost like cured leather, his upper arms, legs, and derriere were pale as the moon.

"Hm," Landrum grunted. "I feel naked as an egg, too. Think the Chiricahua will catch on fast to me, do you?"

"I'll have to go in first anyway," Glidinghawk said. "I know a few words of their lingo. You'll be more useful behind me, anyway. So when I say halt, you hit the ground and stay back from the action. Wait. You might still have a chance to save yourself if this goes wrong."

"Hell, if you are crazy enough to pull this stunt, so am I," Landrum said. "Lead on."

Again, the horses were tethered, this time a quarter of a mile from the Chiricahua camp. By now, the two men dared talk only in whispers. Anything that made noise could put a sleepless brave on the alert.

"I'll walk upright," Glidinghawk said softly. "You follow about five lengths behind me. And say some prayers for me. I'll need them."

Landrum helped Glidinghawk shoulder the dead brave's body. The dead fish were in a leather pouch around Glidinghawk's waist.

"Now," Glidinghawk said.

Landrum lowered himself to the earth. He grunted, bit his lips, and settled into a position from which he could proceed in a gliding crawl. He had fallen on his pistol. It dug into his bare flesh. He had insisted on wearing his holster over his loincloth.

Glidinghawk was armed with his knife and his strong hands—hands that had killed twice tonight. He carried the lance and shield. He hoped the brave he had taken them from did not have any peculiarities of posture or gait that would immediately give him away.

It was awkward going, with the weight of the corpse dragging him down. Glidinghawk gritted his teeth and forced himself forward. Any step could be his last.

The Chiricahua's wickiups were directly ahead, built in a circle around a central point. Their rounded mounds were not so different from the sloping, convex shapes of the surrounding hills. But their outline were hairy rather than smooth around the edges—an illusion created by the willow branches they were made from.

The squaws were the ones who built the wickiups, Glidinghawk knew. These were semi-permanent, sturdy enough to weather a season. Apache construction might seem flimsy—branches, a thatching of buffalo grass or hides walling a wooden frame—but it withstood the elements.

Since this was the hot season, the walls around the bottom of the wickiups were open to catch the breezes. That might be a plus, if Glidinghawk could get to Celia. In winter, there was only one narrow entrance to the dwellings.

Glidinghawk's keen eyes took in the entire layout before searching for how many men were on guard. Each wickiup represented the house of an Apache couple and their unmarried children. The shaman—medicine man or woman—had a wickiup to himself.

Quickly, the disguised Omaha calculated that the 12 dwellings he counted meant upwards of 25 braves. The women and children who might get in the way, he didn't care to count. Unlike hardcase army men who said, "A dead Injun is a dead Injun," Glidinghawk dreaded injuring squaws or their offspring.

"*Ay-ie?*" A voice called.

It was the sentry on the north side of the encampment.

"*Ay-ie*," Glidinghawk called back softly. From this distance, Gerald appeared to be the Apache guard walking in to report something. The next few seconds would be crucial.

Glidinghawk swiftly removed one of the shad from his leather pouch. He laid the stark naked dead man out on the ground. The spot was 20 feet from the sentry, who was wandering over.

Hands shaking but nimble, Glidinghawk tipped the dead man's head back and stuffed the fish in his rigid mouth. Its tail and head extended on either side of the dead man's grimacing lips.

He backed up two paces. He raised his shield. He readied his knife. He let out a low, keening wail—a wail that raised goosebumps on Landrum's skin as he waited behind, clutching the earth.

The other men on guard were instantly alert.

The closest sentry was soon flanked by other braves, whose curiosity was aroused. They came closer. Glidinghawk wailed again. His voice rose like that of a wolf howling at the moon.

The guards crowded in.

The first one stared in disbelief. He recognized the empty husk of his dead brother. He knelt closer—close enough so Glidinghawk was within a hair's breath of stabbing him. Close enough so the superstitious Chiricahua could see the dulled scales of the dreaded fish.

The Apache's scream was blood-curdling.

The others saw it then.

Bad medicine. The worst.

An Apache would take on a den of snakes or go up against a scalping rival band single-handedly before he would come close to a fish.

Fish meant worse than death. Fish meant a death that never ended, an eternity of pursuit by the most evil spirits—more evil than a mere mortal could imagine.

They shrieked. One after the other, as their eyes

were drawn to the fish, they howled in terror. One brave warrior fell over on his side, stiff from fright, passed out cold.

The others scattered in panic.

Women and children cried out from within the wickiups.

Only one man dared challenge Glidinghawk. He came from his dwelling and walked forward while the men around him ran in all directions and wailed. From his royal bearing and the markings on his headband, Glidinghawk knew he was the shaman.

Only the old medicine man could calm his people now. He would have to prove his spirit was stronger. Glidinghawk sensed the danger immediately. The shaman paced quickly to the fish-mouthed corpse.

Sometimes, decisions that take only the blink of an eye seem to roll around in the mind for a year. Glidinghawk saw two paths unfold before him as clearly as if they were visions.

In one, he could brandish his knife and kill the shaman. He could see the blood of his enemy spurting and the momentary thrill of his own triumph. He could also see the arrow that would then fly directly through his heart.

In the other vision, he rendered the shaman powerless and lived to tell the tale.

So when the Chiricahua stepped past the spectacle that had totally unnerved the other braves, Glidinghawk raised not his knife, but the other fish. He had two left.

In order to come forward with a shad in either hand, he would have to drop the shield. Instinctively, he had it held fast over his vulnerable flesh, muscles and sinews.

But even in their abject fright, the other braves were watching. Their eyes skittered toward the dead man, the fish, the shaman, and Glidinghawk walking tall in the moonlight.

Two paces and the shaman's face was close, so close Glidinghawk could see the anger building there. He dropped his protection. He strode forward in a strange, jerky dance. He waved the stinking fish in the shaman's face.

"*Ay-ie!*"

The shaman whirled around and ran after the others.

Glidinghawk saw that squaws and children were joining the men. They ran in circles of panic. It appeared that their numbers were diminishing, heading south outside the circle of the wickiups.

Once they saw the shaman had no medicine to counteract the fish, they were more afraid. They dashed here and there as if pursued by an army of flesh and blood spirits.

Glidinghawk was on the alert.

One man, less superstitious or more educated than the rest, could yet bring the curse of death upon him. He surveyed the scene in a glance. The wickiup in the direct center of camp was the one he wanted.

Repositioning the shield so the front of his body, at least, was protected, he advanced. In his right hand, he still held the biggest weapon of all, the rapidly deteriorating shad. His nostrils flared at the ripe scent.

"*Ay-ie!* Yippee!" he heard Landrum bellow from behind him. The older man came barreling up and slapped Glidinghawk on the shoulder. "Fish. I want my fish."

"Fool!" Glidinghawk hissed, but he handed the white-legged apparition one.

He understood from Landrum's glittering eyes what was happening to both of them. They were acting almost as if drunk, as if the extreme danger and long odds were an elixir coursing through them.

They advanced with Landrum covering Glidinghawk.

They passed a crying child. Landrum whirled with his pistol cocked. He fired. Glidinghawk's heart leapt to his throat—until he saw that Landrum had fired to miss. The child ran away bawling. Later, he would be called One Who Cries at Danger.

The warrior braves were not so lucky as the child.

Landrum shot at least two through the back. The band was now retreating in a disorganized stream. A shot rang out. The bullet nipped Landrum's shoulder. He cursed and stumbled.

Glidinghawk dove down through the open wall of the central wickiup. Speed was essential. Now that traditional weapons were in play, the Apache might have second thoughts about the fish. Not that their terror of the creatures would abate—it was a deep-rooted, gut fear—but they might think to take some enemies with them to a fish-laden hell.

Inside the dwelling, Glidinghawk made out the supine figure of a bound woman. He knew it was Celia from the spill of hair. She was wearing the men's trousers she had dressed in the day before. She was still. Too still. Her head was hanging at an odd angle.

Glidinghawk knelt by her.

Tenderly, he brushed the hair away from her face.

He saw a patch of coagulating blood by her forehead. One of her arms was untied. Someone had been trying to free her when the panic got out of hand. So whoever had been guarding her knocked her over the head. The wound was not pretty.

"Celia!"

His exclamation was almost a plea. She opened her eyes briefly and moved her head. She moaned and fell back into unconsciousness.

Glidinghawk did not have time to be gentle. Outside, shouts and shots rent the air. He heaved her up over his shoulder and, half-crouching, escaped the confines of the wickiup.

Landrum was waiting. By now, his face was ashen. The sun hiding below the horizon was beginning to lighten the sky.

Together, with Celia in Glidinghawk's arms, they ran north the way they had come. Landrum kept looking over his shoulder. Glidinghawk concentrated on making distance with the heavy load he carried.

The quarter mile to the horses seemed much further.

Strange Indian chants echoed from back beyond the camp. Glidinghawk had seen the slight gully south of the Apache stronghold. He had known that was where their horses and beasts of burden would be, in a cul-de-sac.

His acute ears picked up the unshod feet of a small pony manned by a Chiricahuan. They were so close to their own horses now. Only yards to go.

"Landrum!" Glidinghawk shouted, not slowing his pace. "One on horseback coming your way."

Landrum Davis had not heard the approaching warrior. The thud of his own heartbeat had been too strong. He wheeled around and stood his ground.

Over his shoulder, he cried out, "Keep going. I'll handle it. Get out of here."

Racing on foot with the burden of Celia, Glidinghawk could do nothing but obey. He had to reach their own horses before the Chiricahua. He hated to have his back turned, knowing that Landrum might be killed at any second.

Landrum's sorrel Devil pawed the ground, sensing danger the way a good horse does. He was the horse closest to Glidinghawk. The beast strained against his reins and snorted.

Surefoot and Glidinghawk's unnamed gelding were upset, too, but they were further back. Gerald did what he knew he must do. He grasped Devil by the neck and swung around to the other side of him, so both he and Celia were protected by the animal's proud, arched neck.

Glidinghawk's whole body trembled from the strain. He had Celia jammed up against horse flesh. He heard the single shot of a rifle, then the shorter bark of Landrum's Peacemaker.

"Bastard!" Landrum yelled.

Glidinghawk could not see what was happening. But he heard the Apache pony whinny and the battle cry of the lone Chiricahua.

He pressed even closer to Celia's limp but warm body. He had no weapon at hand. He protected her the only way he could, with his body on one side of her, the horse's on the other. With her sandwiched in like that, Glidinghawk waited and prayed.

Now, in a direct line, were Landrum, the advancing Apache brave, Devil, Celia and Glidinghawk, who closed his eyes and willed himself to endure for however long it took.

It was not easy to stand there, helpless, fighting the quivering horse, the weight of the woman he wanted more than anything to save, and the overwhelming fear of his own death.

When he heard the next rifle shot and felt the spooked gelding startle, convulse and fall to the ground, it was almost a relief. He tugged Celia backward and her body fell on top of his—just in time. Another second, and she would have been crushed by the weight of the dead horse.

Glidinghawk lay on his back, staring up into Celia's unconscious face. He was barely aware of Landrum's killing shot tumbling the Chiricahua from his fleeing mount.

CHAPTER SIX

Landrum ran over, cursing and shouting.

The first sight of Glidinghawk and Celia was alarming—until Glidinghawk shouted, "Help me with Celia. We've got to get out of here!"

Wiping tears of fear and frustration from his dusty cheek, Landrum knelt down and gently lifted his female teammate from Glidinghawk's prone body.

He prodded her wounded forehead with a gentle finger. Landrum's own shoulder nick blazed painfully, but he was far more concerned about Celia's concussion.

Glidinghawk sat up. "We only have two horses now. Do you want to ride Celia with you, or should I take her?"

"You'd better," Landrum said. "My arm is stiffer than a man on a three day drunk. I'll get the saddlebags from Devil. I hope that appaloosa can handle the weight. That gold is heavy."

Landrum stroked Celia's pale face while Glidinghawk transferred the gold and canteens to Surefoot, Celia's horse. He found a rope to tie Celia behind him on his own horse. They would have to ride hard.

The Chiricahua band had been thoroughly spooked, but the fact that one man dared to ride against them meant that others, too, might find a reserve of courage.

Besides, by now the relentless sun was pushing up over the horizon. Daylight would give the warriors courage.

They worked swiftly. Landrum grunted, groaned and sweat beads of pain helping Celia up into the saddle behind Glidinghawk. Then he mounted Surefoot and spurred the horse forward, due north, to where the mules had been tied.

Glidinghawk clucked his tongue and his gelding followed along. The situation, he knew, was not good. Celia was bouncing and moaning—at least that was a sign of life. Landrum's wound was on his right shoulder, and made it difficult for him to ride, much less shoot.

Worse, Glidinghawk had washed and packed his knife wound from yesterday, the one on his back ribs, but it was swollen and oozing with pus. He did not want to mention it to Landrum, but Glidinghawk was deeply concerned about his own health.

Already, although the heat shimmered up from the desert hardpan, Glidinghawk was shivering with chill. Moments later, his entire body was on fire. Then the chills racked him again.

The three of them, miraculously, were alive and free, but there wasn't an able-bodied man—or woman—among them.

They needed to ride far enough from danger to make camp. But how far was that? The three miles to where they had left the mules seemed an eternity—and there was no way the two overburdened horses could keep up that loping gait in the daytime heat.

For a long time, the men rode without speaking. Glidinghawk saw Landrum take a long suck on his canteen. He was tempted himself. The world was becoming hazy and dry. He could almost feel the cool water sliding down his parched throat. But he chewed on some willow bark instead.

It was the Indian way. The bark was bitter and medicinal, starting a flow of saliva in his mouth. Once they got to the mules, Glidinghawk promised himself, once they were assured of their water supply, he would drink long and deeply.

But they rode on without finding the mules.

Instead, they saw tracks.

Tracks leading away from the boulders and toward the mountains. Someone had discovered the mules. Someone had taken them.

By now, Glidinghawk was not sure his judgment was good. His face burned with fever. The chills rattled through him. It seemed only Celia's limp body anchored him to the saddle.

Landrum dismounted and scanned the ground.

Glidinghawk asked, "Are you sure this was the spot?"

Landrum looked at the Omaha oddly. "Yes, of course I'm sure. We tied them ourselves. There—see the tracks."

Glidinghawk shrugged, shook his head from side to side, and said, "Just wanted to make sure. These could have been someone else's pack mules. They were ours, were they?"

"You know damned well they were!" Landrum exploded. "What's wrong with you?"

"Just checking," Glidinghawk said briefly.

"Checking my ass," Landrum said, drawing closer to his two mounted friends. Celia was sagging against Glidinghawk's back. The Indian and Landrum were still dressed in their Apache disguises. Glidinghawk's bared skin was glistening with sweat, and under the bronze tone of his skin was a greenish pallor.

Landrum's nose wrinkled up. He smelled something. Perhaps from the fish, he thought—only the scent was sweetly rotten. He looked up at the front of Celia's shirt.

Something was very wrong.

Another wound they hadn't seen? Celia's shirt was damp. A pinkish, rank liquid stained the front of the fabric. Landrum pushed her roughly back several inches to examine it more closely.

Then he realized that both the odor and the stain had come from Glidinghawk. Landrum shuddered. The stinging ache in his upper shoulder was nothing. Celia had a fair chance of coming out of her concussion.

But Landrum had seen infected wounds before.

His mind flashed back to a cousin of his who had died in his arms. The battle of Shiloh, one of many. The wound was nothing, his cousin had told him.

That night, safely behind Confederate lines, Landrum Davis had watched his cousin die.

Landrum had smelled the boy's death before it came. Had seen the inflamed flesh eat away the spirit and life and brightness in his cousin's eyes.

Now, he looked directly into Glidinghawk's black fathomless eyes. "You are bad sick," he said. "Don't deny it. A lot of good it will do to play hero and then fall off your horse. Do you understand me?"

Another chill shook Glidinghawk's body. He leaned forward over the gelding's neck. He tried to straighten.

"We've come this far," Landrum said grimly. "I'll take the reins and lead. First shade we find, we stay put until nightfall. Looks like I'm going to have to play sawbones to the two of you. Just don't fight me."

"Yes, sir," Glidinghawk mumbled.

Glidinghawk, later, was not sure just when Landrum took over. He recalled the escape from the Apache's summer camp and the dead horse and the Chiricahua falling upward into the air. Vaguely, he remembered heading north to retrieve the mules.

Then memory went blank.

As he was led—along with Celia, who later had about as much memory of the trip as he did—Glidinghawk dreamed of other times and other places.

Although the bright orb in the sky radiated sheer, hellish heat, Glidinghawk dreamt of being cold, so cold that in winter his toes froze to the ground. So cold that his heart was frozen numb when his parents died.

In his fevered fantasy, Glidinghawk was a boy again, being led to an Omaha ceremony by his tribe's old and revered shaman. The medicine man had laid his gnarled hands on the boy. Those hands were the twisted, rough roots of an old oak tree, strong and life giving, sucking up the vibrations of life from the boy.

The shaman was not a bad one. He tried to lead his people. He did not use their beliefs to further his own power, as so many from the other tribes did. He had named the Indian child Glidinghawk, after laying his hands on the youth's head and feeling the future there.

"This one will not live as other Indians," the old man had told his people. "He will glide like the hawk and see many things that we have never dreamed of. He will be a bird of prey, but a wise bird who crosses mountains and plains and knows only the wind for a friend."

In his dream, Glidinghawk smiled. His people were all listening closely and nodding their heads. Glidinghawk was proud that he would be different and travel far past the mountains and plains.

"But this boy, this Glidinghawk, shall have much pain from seeing too much. He will be saddened because he can see the autumn of his people and not their spring. He will be cut off from his Indian brothers, a hawk on the wind . . ."

And so it was, when his parents died, and the missionaries took him in, tried to make a model Christian of him. So it was when he went to the big university many mountains away. And the predictions of the shaman were beaten out of him.

A hawk on the wind, gliding now above the conflict and pain, melting into the stream of death. Almost—until he felt a jarring pain that seared deep into his flesh. He felt drops of liquid wash over his face.

Perhaps, though, it was only his tears as he dreamed of how he used to feel, really feel the pain and the joy of life so many years ago.

Finally, he heard a human voice.

A woman's voice.

"His fever has broken. He will have a deep scar, but the rotten smell is gone. If we can find water, he might live."

A deeper male voice answered. "How is your head? And I need an honest answer. I have to decide where we are going to go from here. Tell me the worst."

"I guess . . . it comes and goes. It aches, and it's hard

to do things, like make my fingers do what I want them to. Sometimes, I feel fuzzy. But it's better."

It took Glidinghawk a long time to know who these people were. At first, he tried to sink back into his dream, but it was gone, washed away by the voices of white people. He let their voices drone on. He kept his eyes shut.

Landrum . . . Celia . . . the names echoed in his brain. The hands he felt soothing him were Celia's and the gruff, drawling voice belonged to Landrum. He was back somewhere with them . . . Fort Griffin?"

No, that did not seem right, although there was something that came to him about a night on the trail, when they had been as close to him as any two people on earth.

His eyelids opened.

It was twilight and the world looked strange. Shapes seemed to move, to waver in the dusk. The land was a flash of dun-colored rock, barren and inhospitable, touched by flashes of rose.

Arizona Territory.

Slavers and Chiricahua.

Dead fish.

Glidinghawk opened his eyes fully and tried to sit up. "We made it?" he asked.

Landrum came over to his side. He supported his friend's back and his left arm. Celia was on the other side of Glidinghawk, wiping his face clumsily with a handkerchief.

Glidinghawk blinked rapidly. Celia was openly weeping—later, she would say the blow on her head did strange things to her control over her emotions.

Landrum turned so his prominent nose was outlined

like a cypher. He rubbed his eyes. "Damned dust in my eye," he said. It was moments before he could speak.

"I think we will be fine, now that you are back with us," Landrum said. "We have two horses and half a canteen of water left. If we ride through the night we might find water. It's touch and go with Celia, but I think she'll make it. It's you we weren't so sure of."

"I'll be fine," Glidinghawk answered. Then, biting his lips, he added, "Thanks . . . for sticking with me."

"Only thing I hate worse than an Indian who thinks he's a hero," Landrum grumbled, "is a dead Indian hero. Think you can ride or do we have to strap you up?"

"I can ride better than some ex-Confederate greenhorns I know," Glidinghawk said.

It was getting sticky. Both men backed away from the revelation; they truly cared for each other, as more than working partners on a dangerous mission.

Celia, too, sniffled, blew her nose, and declared, "Let's go."

They mounted up. This time Celia rode with Landrum on the gelding and Glidinghawk rode with the load of gold, on Celia's appaloosa. They did not try for any of these could disable a horse and throw its rider. night held danger.

A hidden rock, a somnolent rattler, a gopher hole — any of these could disable a horse ands throw its riders. So they settled into the rhythm of a slow canter.

It jarred Glidinghawk. He felt an empty spot where his knife wound had been, where once there had been flesh and muscle sheathing his bone.

Landrum, in desperation, had mixed the white medicine man's crystals with some of the last water in his canteen. The crystals had turned into a deep purple liquid that burned away the rotting, infected flesh.

Then he had repacked the wound with the Indian herbs Glidinghawk swore by and bandaged Glidinghawk's back. He had tended to his own wound, too. Landrum still found it almost impossible to move his arm freely, but it was painful rather than serious.

Landrum hated playing sawbones, but he knew how. He had seen enough combat to know that surviving a fight was only the first part of the battle. He respected the Indian's herbal knowledge — up to a point.

When it came to serious doctoring, Landrum believed that anything that hurt enough to make a grown man of cry or pass out just might work.

Unfortunately, he also knew enough to be pretty damned worried about his charges. Celia could take a bad turn at any minute, and Glidinghawk needed lots of water if he was to heal up and throw off the last of the ravaging fever.

Glidinghawk was stoic. Landrum knew the Indian would make no complaint, would ride on until they stopped, hurting and hazy in the head but brave about it.

Celia was brave, too, but she moaned from time to time — and there wasn't a thing Landrum could do about it. They could all die out here.

And, once again, Landrum felt the full weight of being senior operative. Celia did not know enough about surviving in the wild to be of much help, and Glidinghawk was too sick to make decisions.

So the decisions rested in Landrum's hands, and he wasn't at all sure he was up to guessing right himself. The only thing guiding him now was the thought of the stronghold in the Gila Mountains.

Too bad you can't drink gold, Landrum thought. *Then I would not need help to save my friends.*

But the only slight chance Landrum could see was reaching the bandelero's mountain hideout. What was that Mex slaver's name, Sexto Diaz? Then they could buy some recuperating time. Gold for water and safety. At the moment, it seemed like a fair trade.

Still, Landrum was not about to tell Celia and Glidinghawk what was in the back of his mind. They had enough to deal with without the added strain of knowing.

Landrum chuckled mirthlessly.

What was it his grandmother used to say? Out of the frying pan into the fire? Maybe Glidinghawk was smart enough to think of a better solution, but he was out of commission for the moment. And damned if Landrum could.

So, unless by some miracle they happened on a source of food, water and shelter, Landrum had to figure that their best bet was riding toward the slaver camp.

Then it would be touch and go.

With gold and lies and a whole lot of brass, all three of them might live to tell the tale.

At that same moment, Sexto Diaz was celebrating.

He had brought a shipment of tequila back from his trip to Sonora—Sonora, Mexico, rather than the town of the same name across the border in United States territory.

Sexto had triumphed again. That last shipment of

Apache maidens had brought top peso—especially the beautiful squaw who called herself Saguaro Flower.

She was special.

Sexto had sold her to an old man who wished to cure his impotence with the soft, tender flesh of a young and nubile maiden. The old goat.

The price the old man offered was high. Sexto wanted to go at her himself, but for once he put business first. He wondered if her virgin blood had been spilled yet on the bedsheets of old Manuel Rodriguez.

Now, after a few days in his Gila Mountain hideout celebrating with his men, Sexto would contact his crooked army friends.

He would buy more slaves cheap, sell them high down south across the border, and be richer than he was today.

His broad, peasant face broke into a drunken laugh. He was a swarthy man of enormous appetites for whiskey, wealth and women.

Life was rich, and it would be richer still tonight.

One of his men had found some pack mules on the trip back. The man's name was Jaime. Sexto never liked the man, but he was his wife's good-for-nothing brother. Jaime claimed that the mules now belonged to him.

Sexto had held his tongue. He did not disagree with Jaime, only let the man proudly care for the mules and bring them back into the mountains.

Then Sexto had broken out the tequila that glowed like a warm fire in his rounded belly.

Jaime was already quite drunk, but not so drunk that he could not feel the beating that he had coming to him for daring to believe that any spoils belonged to anyone other than Sexto Diaz, his leader.

True, beating Jaime was not as satisfying as slashing the clear, soft skin of a woman, but it would do. Sexto felt a tingle of anticipation in his hands.

Life was indeed rich, when a day brought fresh mules and the chance to administer a beating.

CHAPTER SEVEN

Landrum realized they were traveling blindly. He had a general idea of the direction he was leading them in, but that was all. His own head began to flash visions of mountains and streams, but they were not the arid rock formations, mountains or thin trickles of this region.

Night in the desert area is deceptively sharp and clear. Again tonight, there was a moon out. Yet Landrum could not tell if the vague outlines he saw up ahead indicated the foothills of the Gilas, or only his imagination.

Celia clung to his back, her head resting uncomfortably on his right shoulder. Last time he had halted to check on her, she appeared to be dozing.

Glidinghawk was slumped in his saddle, letting Surefoot carry him. Appaloosas had a reputation for being reliable and hardy, but after hours of monotonous travel the animal seemed to be tiring. The saddlebags filled with gold weighed far more than the extra weight of Celia that Landrum carried.

They no longer cantered.

Walking was pace enough for the beasts. It was plodding going. One minute, Landrum was sure they were close to their destination, the next, it seemed to slide further and further away.

Soon, they would have to make camp, water or no water. If they could find a place protected from the sun and sleep out the day, they could again travel in the relative cool of the night.

If they did not become too weak from thirst and hunger, that is. A while back, Landrum had tried to get his charges — that was how he thought of them, now that Celia and Glidinghawk were sick — to chew some beef jerky.

Celia had put a piece up to her mouth. At this point, she was reacting like a sleepwalker, or a cow placidly, unquestioningly chewing her cud.

"Don't make her eat," Glidinghawk had ordered.

Glidinghawk had pushed the hard, salty beef away from her flushed face. It fell on the ground. "It will make her thirsty. Better to be hungry."

Landrum felt helpless.

Sure, he should have known better, but he wasn't thinking. So Glidinghawk, sick as he was, had to intervene. Beef jerky was not smart. It looked like another long, dry day coming up.

Perhaps Landrum should test Glidinghawk out, see if the Indian could think of a better plan than walking right into the bandelero's camp. If only the three of them had several days to rest up and get well, riding into the lion's den would not be necessary.

Weighing the pros and cons kept Landrum going.

He was having a running argument in his head. Every step the horse took, it seemed, Landrum would think of another reason they needed other men to help them—even bad men.

Every other step, his mind went around in opposite circles, trying to think of a way around it. Soon, if they kept going, it would be too late.

But first things first. As the night sky turned a clear, lead gray, Landrum thought he spotted salvation.

Distances out here could not be measured by a man's eye. That mesa up ahead looked so close Landrum felt like he could reach out and touch it, but he knew damned well it had to be five miles away at least. Even so, he was sure he saw a patch of vegetation by its base.

He spurred his horse until he was side by side with Glidinghawk. The Indian's eyes were glazed over, but he turned in Landrum's direction.

"Do you think that's an oasis up there?" Landrum asked.

He could see that it took Glidinghawk great effort to focus. "Even if it isn't it will have to do," Glidinghawk said. "I can't ride much further. Whatever it is, it'll give some shade."

So they speeded up.

Surefoot and the unnamed gelding responded to the spurring, but it was a valiant effort. They needed water almost as much as the men.

Landrum recalled saloon talk of the now discarded army plan to import camels to the desert; a band of camels had been brought over to the American southwest, but the Civil War had stopped the experiment.

Landrum wished he was on camelback now. Those

beasts could survive for weeks without water. Another day and the three of them would be without horses.

The miles seemed endless.

Then Landrum let out a loud whoop. He wheeled around and shouted, "Water!"

The thirsty beasts, sensing relief, gave a last burst of speed. Glidinghawk vaguely saw the algae-scummed pond at the foot of the mesa. Cacti of different shapes, some tall and twisted, grew nearby, but no trees.

Surefoot jiggled Glidinghawk to full consciousness, rushing toward the spot.

Landrum's elation was like a live force coursing through him. He had gone without sleep for over 48 hours. He had held the lives of Celia and Glidinghawk in his hands. He had been afraid he would fail them. And here it was—water!

"Halt! Goddammit, stop!" Glidinghawk called hoarsely.

But it was too late.

The mount that Landrum and Celia rode was right in the puddle lapping up the water—water poisoned by the minerals of the desert rocks. The bleached skeleton of a man and his mule protruded from the sandy bank.

Celia was trying to struggle down to the small pond.

Awakened from her uneasy doze, all she could see— or think about—was a drink. Slyly and quickly, she ignored Landrum as she wriggled from the back of the saddle.

Glidinghawk, who had cautiously stopped further back, slipped from Surefoot's back in a burst of speed. He tied the nickering horse securely to a rock, and rushed to catch Celia before it was too late.

Landrum turned in his saddle and struggled with her, too, but she slipped from his grasp. She was plunging into the wetness when Glidinghawk spun her around and carted her to the bank, still kicking.

She cried like a little girl whose toy has been taken away. "I want a drink of water," she said plaintively.

"That stuff is pure poison," Glidinghawk said. He was extremely weak, but a shot of adrenaline kept him going. He managed to shout, "Get that horse out of there, Landrum. Maybe we can save him."

Landrum pulled back on the bridle. The gelding reared up and pawed. The animal cut his lips straining against the reins, pulling. He had a taste of moisture and he wanted more.

Landrum spurred and whipped, but it took him several wheeling turns to bring the gelding under control. Surefoot, watching, also pawed the ground and whinnied piteously.

Glidinghawk, still tugging at Celia, backed into the rocks and sat. He no longer had the strength to stand. His knees had threatened to buckle under him.

Landrum wearily joined them after tying his protesting horse away from the deadly oasis. They sat. The sun rose. Landrum wiped his brow. His piercing eyes were staring straight ahead, at nothing.

Finally, he said, "What now? I guess I'm not fit to lead a pack of jackasses."

Glidinghawk did not argue. He was glad last night's decisions had not been on his back. And now it was too late for him. He felt his body weaken minute by minute.

Still, through sheer instinct, his mind was rolling

around the possibilities, hovering around their problems like a bird looking for a place to light.

Celia's tears had dried, but she looked and acted like she was back in another world. Something in her mind had jarred or snapped; in time, she might snap out of it. For now, she was like a five-year-old child. She would have to be protected.

Landrum, physically, was the strongest of the three at the moment, but Glidinghawk could see the older man was suffering from lack of sleep as well as lack of nourishment.

Right now, Glidinghawk would not give a plug nickel for his own chances, but he had already resigned himself to dying out here.

If only he could force himself to move and act for the next few hours, the other two might stand a chance.

"Landrum," he said slowly, but Davis was almost asleep.

"Can I help?" Celia said. The years of her growing up had faded away. Her voice was wispy. Her eyes, too, had a vacant look. Their brilliant emerald color glittered like gems without any human spirit behind them.

"Yes, you can help," Glidinghawk said gently. "I want you to stay with Landrum while he sleeps, here in the shade."

A flicker of suspicion showed on her face. "That's all?" she said, her tone high and querulous.

"Yes. It's like a game," Glidinghawk said. Damn, this would be easier if she was herself, if the effects from the blow on her head had not come back. "I will tie you up and you close your eyes until I come back. He's going to play, too. I'll tie the other end of the rope to him."

Glidinghawk shook Landrum, who came out of his trance, rubbing his eyes hopelessly. "Wha . . . sorry. I fell asleep."

"That's just what you have to do. Sleep," Glidinghawk said. "I want you to move closer to the rocks, so you'll have some shade. Celia's out of her mind, at least right now. We can't trust her to stay put. So I'm going to tie her to you, so she doesn't go for the water again."

"And you?" Landrum asked.

"I'll sleep later. First, I have some things to do. I won't go far—you can be sure of that."

"And the horses?" Landrum asked.

Glidinghawk had been thinking of them. He needed to get them into the shade. Or Surefoot, anyway. The rising sun was heating the earth like an oven.

The men looked at the beasts now. The gelding was bellowing and lying down. Foam flecked his mouth. "We have to shoot him," Glidinghawk said. "I'll bring Surefoot over here. We have no choice. I'll do it. You sleep."

Landrum was going to protest that the shot might attract human prey, as well as vultures. But he thought better of it.

Instead, Landrum nodded, his mouth too dry for speech. He understood as well as the Indian that they could not be worse off than they were right now. And he could not move until he got some sleep.

"Ow," Celia said, as Glidinghawk roped her ankle and tied the other end of the rope around Landrum's middle. "I don't like this game."

"Neither do I," Glidinghawk said, looking deeply into her eyes. For a moment, he saw recognition there, an instant of understanding.

He rose quickly and strode away.

He untied Surefoot and led the appaloosa to the pitifully small patch of shade. Landrum was already sleeping like the dead. Glidinghawk was glad to see it. Celia was cuddling into his body, weeping.

Glidinghawk took the rifle. The gelding he had acquired at Fort Lowell watched him approach. The beast's eyeballs rolled over white in pain. He had been a sturdy, dependable horse.

Glidinghawk had refused to name him. In this business, on undercover missions, Glidinghawk had steeled himself not to get close to man or beast. They would too soon fade out of his life, leaving only the pain.

But Glidinghawk had gotten close to Landrum and Celia. They were a part of him as if they were his blooded family. And for a time, this gelding had been a part of him and served him well.

He sighted the rifle barrel.

"I name you One Whose Spirit Is Set Free," Glidinghawk whispered softly.

He squeezed the trigger.

The shot rang out.

Its echo whistled back from the mountains many miles away. Most of the bandeleros there were still sleeping off the potent liquor they had consumed last night.

Jaime, the man who had been brutally beaten by Sexto Diaz, heard the sound. He was in too much pain to sleep, but he smiled.

He hoped there were men out there who would bring vengeance down on his master. He could not. His sister was married to the fat slave trader, but even she would be better off without him.

Jaime had prayed to the Virgin about it. Perhaps this shot was a sign that his prayers would be answered. He hoped the others had not heard the shot. He would not report it.

The gelding gave a last dying bellow and rolled over. Its swift legs kicked the air and were still. Glidinghawk heaved the rifle, butt first, back in the direction of the others. He could put it away properly later. He got out his knife.

It was time to cut some cactus.

Glidinghawk had been far busier than either Landrum or Celia when they were supplying at the army garrison. He had spent long nights listening to the Apache scouts talk of surviving in this wilderness.

He walked slowly down to the poisoned oasis. Idly, he studied the bones of the dead man and his mule. Soon, One Whose Spirit Is Set Free would be like them, whitened bones picked clean by the carrion, dried by the sun.

The thought strengthened Glidinghawk's resolve.

He would not let Landrum and Celia end up like that.

With the last of his strength, Glidinghawk carefully set about cutting the cacti. There was a good selection, cholla with their delicate tendrils and tiny red flowers, barrel cactus as globular as melons, the cochineals with big stalks and smaller globes, and prickly pear.

Glidinghawk was not used to this task. The barbs stung his hands. He was not sure which plants yielded the most moisture.

Still, he knew he must gather the leathery lobes, pull out the barbs, and strip the tough, leathery outer skin of the cacti.

Inside would be the moist, fleshy membranes.

Inside was the key to surviving one more day.

As he worked, Glidinghawk hummed tunelessly. Perhaps, after he sent Landrum and Celia on without him, refreshed by sleep and the juice of the cacti, he might survive another day himself.

Sending them off without him . . . it was the only way. He had managed to keep going today, but his body felt as if it were strained to the limit. The wound in his back ached dully, except when a sudden movement shot stabbing pain through him.

But it was the weakness he could not fight. He thought his fever was gone now, but all he wanted to do was sleep. He knew his own limitations. He knew he had gone past them.

With two horses, they might have struggled on together. But now there was only one horse — and that one suffering from dehydration.

Glidinghawk slashed another cactus stem. The horse would need some moist, life-giving pulp, too. His hand was dotted with pinpricks of blood.

Once the others rode off, Glidinghawk promised himself, he would make another harvest for himself — after he got some sleep. At least he would get to sleep in the cool of night while the others rode on.

When Glidinghawk discovered the clutch of cactus wren eggs nestled in the base of a barrel cactus, his heart sang within him.

It was an omen: there might be a future after all . . . for all of them.

CHAPTER EIGHT

"Goddamnit, I am not leaving you here!" Landrum shouted.

"You must come with us," Celia told Glidinghawk. "We are a team—all three of us. We have to stick together."

The sleep seemed to have brought Celia back to reality, but she wasn't too happy about it. She had gagged over swallowing the raw bird eggs, embryos and all. When the Omaha told Landrum and Celia he was staying right here while they traveled on, she became more agitated.

But Glidinghawk's stoic Indian mask was firmly in place. He squatted beside the mesa, a stone figure, intractable. "The two of you have a chance without me. If you make it, send help. Now go . . . or all three of us will die."

Landrum stood up to his full height and turned his face away, brooding. Neither threats nor blasphemy would change Glidinghawk's mind.

Most frustrating of all, Landrum knew that the

Omaha was right. Leaving Glidinghawk behind to fend for himself was the best decision. The only one possible.

Silently, Landrum prepared the horse for the journey. He checked the stirrups and the saddlebags. He tucked the remainder of the cactus harvest in an oilskin. That, along with the deep sleep he had gotten, had restored Landrum.

At the last minute, he dropped the extra rifle and a small pouch of gold by Glidinghawk's side, alongside the discarded saddle of the gelding they had killed.

Glidinghawk looked up and said, "No speeches."

Landrum's drawn face was difficult to read. The saber scar across his cheek stood out in bas-relief. His appearance was arresting rather than warm or friendly. The warmth came from deep within him.

"We will meet again, brother," he said.

He turned quickly on his heel and mounted Surefoot, beckoning for Celia to follow. He sat tall and rigid in the saddle, his gaze unwavering.

Impulsively, Celia ran back to Glidinghawk, knelt down, and kissed him fully on the lips. Her own were chapped and dry. Her cheek was wet.

Glidinghawk could taste the salt of her tears as he saw Celia and Landrum become smaller and smaller as they headed toward the mountains.

"May all the gods be with you," he whispered.

From time to time, Landrum had felt a deep thirst for whiskey, a burning desire to get to the getting-place and have a drink.

But it was nothing compared to the obsession he felt now for a big, cool drink of water. The cactus pulp had slaked his thirst some—enough so he knew he wasn't about to dry up and turn to dust—but he wanted water more than he could ever remember wanting anything, including a woman.

Water . . . even the muddy Brazos back in Texas sounded so good Landrum knew that he could wallow in it, swallow it all up, spit out the mud and beg for more.

He wished he could stop thinking about it, but mile after plodding mile, that's all that danced in his head. Hell, he'd thrown away bath water he'd give this whole load of gold to drink right now.

Surefoot must be thinking of water too. The poor horse was carrying quite a load and he'd been bone dry until Glidinghawk fixed him up with some cactus juice. Juice? It was pulp and it tasted bitter but it had been wet.

How long could a man go without water?

He had to get his mind on something else. So he turned and asked Celia, "You all right?"

Stupid question. She was alive, but about half the time she was someplace else. Landrum almost hoped that she stayed there, too, because he wasn't too sure about right now.

"I want a drink. Please let me have some water. I'll be good. Just give me a drink," she begged.

"A little while longer, Cel, and we'll have a big drink," he promised.

And then called himself a liar.

It seemed that the terrain was changing slightly, that

it was getting higher. Or maybe the air just seemed thinner. Maybe if they climbed high enough, they'd run smack into a wet cloud.

Water. It got so he could feel and taste it. Except every time Landrum tried to swallow, his throat was choked and gritty. The whole inside of his mouth felt as if it had been hung out to dry two cloudless weeks ago.

The only good thing about thinking so much on water, it kept him from thinking about Glidinghawk. Back there. Alone.

The way it had to be, Landrum knew. Surefoot's foreleg caught in a slight depression and he staggered before plodding on. There was no way the horse could have carried three of them.

Landrum had a pocket watch but it had quit. He had no idea what time it was. *Half past watering time,* he thought. Or was that three hours ago?

He believed they were heading due north. If the maps and his reckoning were right, that should be leading them to the Gila foothills, where that Mexican had his camp. He'd bet they had plenty of water — and food — and knew the territory. He bet they had whiskey, too. But first, he wanted a cool, big drink of water.

Water . . . the taste of it coming out of a canteen was tinny, a little like the way metal smelled, but it wasn't bad. Yes, he could go for some canteen water right now, even if it was tepid and musty.

Now, river water had that clay taste to it, sort of made your teeth ache, but there was some full-bodied flavor to it. It wouldn't be Landrum's first choice, but he wouldn't say no.

Landrum never realized how many different kinds of

water there were, never gave it much thought. Well, maybe once, where they had those sulphur springs in the Texas hill country. Smelled like rotten eggs, but it went down the throat as cool and silky as a whore's French undergarments felt against the skin.

Pure spring water . . . now that was something a man could kill for. Some folks said it didn't have any taste, but they were wrong. It tasted clear and clean as crystal, only better, wetter. It was sweet without being sugary. Cool without being cold. Now, that was choice.

"Landrum, what's that up ahead?" Celia asked, pointing.

He wanted to tell her not to bother him. He just about tasted that pure, spring water he was thinking about. Besides, there wasn't too much to see out there, just mile after mile of endless scrub leading slightly up—

"—Whoa!"

Landrum pulled back the reins. The horse stopped and started to sink down. Directly ahead was a steep drop. A ravine—a gorge!

Jumping down, Landrum walked to the edge. Two more paces, and they would have gone over. He had to start concentrating. Unless his eyes were deceiving him, there was the thin trickle of a stream down there. There was a reflective shimmer of moonlight far below.

The only problem was getting from here to there, and it looked tricky. So far, they had been traveling a gradual incline, so gradual that except for the strain and the thinning air it didn't seem like they were climbing.

Now, Landrum realized they had reached their

goal — or maybe overshot it. Now, they would have to find a way down and around to the stream. They had gone far north of the Gila San Francisco, so if luck was with them, this was an offshoot of the Black River.

It was too dangerous to tackle at night, now that the land surrounding them was pitted with erosions and cliffs and surprises like the sheer drop right in front of them.

They would have to sit tight until daybreak.

But then — water.

It was a miracle. If they could only hold on, they would live. Better yet, they might have some options. They might even be able to get up to Fort Apache and get help for Glidinghawk.

Landrum was not a religious man, but he almost felt like getting on his knees in thanksgiving.

"Was there something?" Celia asked.

Her voice was dull and lifeless — but it was hers, the Celia he knew, not the voice of a lost and plaintive child. Why she had come back to herself in time to save them, Landrum could not guess. He only felt very, very grateful.

"A steep drop — and a stream down below. We can't risk it in the dark. Let's make a cold camp and chew some more of those wonderful cactus lobes."

"As long as you don't try to force any more birds' eggs on me," Celia answered.

Daylight found them struggling down a steep, winding path strewn with rocks. They walked it one step at a time, leading the horse. Surefoot could no longer carry them.

"I'm going to roll in it, splash in it, drink it, bathe in it," Celia said.

"Just don't use it all up," Landrum said.

Celia would have said more, but her mouth puckered. She had also been thinking about water all night. Her head ached, fiercely at times, at others dully, but she felt that a good drink of water would cure her.

Landrum quieted. In the back of his mind, there was still the fear; he remembered the poisoned oasis. But the more they descended, the more this looked like a genuine stream.

The path narrowed as it took them around a bend. Landrum was too eager to notice that the way down was worn and had been much used by men. He never thought to question it.

They were about 12 feet above the shimmering promise of water. Surefoot's tongue was protruding from his mouth, fat and swollen. Landrum knew that he couldn't let the horse drink too much too soon, or the animal would bloat.

In fact, Landrum knew that he could not let either Celia or himself drink too much all at once, even if the water was sweet. They could drink a little, lie in it, drink a little more, and it would still be there.

Surefoot nickered and jerked back. He lowered his head and stared down. Then, quivering, he took an eager step to the left.

The reins jerked back in Landrum's hands. He wheeled around, tugging at them.

The horse's hind leg was sliding off the path. His front legs scrabbled frantically for purchase. Landrum pulled with all his might.

Almost in slow motion, Surefoot sank further and further back. His other hind leg was slipping off the rocky ledge. They were so close to the bottom, but the drop could kill. Landrum tugged fiercely and the beast became more panicked.

Celia had been walking ahead.

She turned back and horror flooded through her. Landrum's cruel grip on the rawhide was going to force the horse to back up off the edge — and drag Landrum along with him. Celia's narrowed green eyes took in the edge of the winding path and Landrum's tensed back.

She forgot how much her head ached and her body cried out for water. Forcing the words through a throat raspy with thirst, she said, "Easy . . . easy there . . . Landrum . . . stop pulling . . . that's a boy, Surefoot . . . hold on there, boy . . ."

Celia made a clucking, encouraging noise from deep in her throat. Landrum, startled at first, quelled his own angry grappling. He still held the reins, but he allowed the horse to draw back slightly without his bit digging into his mouth.

Surefoot turned large, limped eyes on Celia. His nostrils quivered. His ears seemed to strain in the direction of her soothing voice. His hind right leg was still sinking into the void, throwing the weight of his haunches toward the fall, but once he quit struggling the shift in balance was not so abrupt.

The main thing Celia had to do was stop the panicking — that could topple them all over the edge. Below Surefoot's sinking leg, Celia saw a slight niche. The horse could never be guided to use it, she knew.

But if she could get down there, she might help Surefoot make the one steady step that would lead him back to safety.

Landrum had frozen, unsure of how to proceed. At least he was not making matters worse any more, as he had been. He felt the fool, standing there as if the thin strips of leather he held could lift a horse. And more the fool because Celia had been the one to stop him.

Landrum felt Celia's hand dig into his back pocket. At first, he couldn't figure it, but then she carefully extracted his handkerchief and eased along the edge to Surefoot's neck.

A blind. Of course.

Maneuvering with difficulty, Celia tied the handkerchief across Surefoot's eyes, all the while speaking gently to him. She was good with horses, Landrum knew. But he had never imagined how good.

Once the scene was shut out, Surefoot calmed a fraction more, enough so that Celia could lower herself down the ledge. Landrum wanted to stop her, to shout at her to let the horse fall, but he knew it would do no good.

Crouching into the rock, hugging it so close that her cheek was up against the hard stone, Celia leaned to one side, so her shoulder was edging up to Surefoot's hoof.

Landrum reacted, trying to slow his movements and his words. He understood that he must lead rather than tug brutally at the horse. His voice had to sound like the cool, calm voice of command.

Inside, Landrum was shaking worse than a cowboy after an end-of-the-trail binge. He was terrified—not of losing the horse, but of losing Celia. What she was doing was dangerous and foolhardy.

"Come on, boy," Landrum said.

He saw the errant hoof make contact with Celia's shoulder, which felt to the animal like a solid base. It might work, if the damned beast would throw his weight on his left foot now.

Otherwise, Celia would never be able to sustain the weight. She would be knocked off her precarious perch, or at the very least crippled.

"Steady boy, easy now," Landrum said.

His words seemed to stretch out.

With great dignity, Surefoot shifted his weight to his front legs and solid back leg and allowed himself to be led back squarely onto the path.

When his right foot lifted up away from Celia, a dizzying relief swept through her. She had not allowed herself to look down. She was afraid of heights.

Landrum advanced, leading the horse, another five paces. Another five steps, and he saw Celia crawl back over the edge.

By the time they reached the bottom, Celia was shaking so hard she could barely manage to swallow the first glorious mouthful of fresh water.

Deeper into the mountains, Sexto Diaz was waking up. He was in a foul mood. Last night had been rich, but this morning his mouth had a sour taste to it, and there was a greasy film of sweat on his swarthy skin.

He looked around at his men — men, hah! Useless turds.

Jaime wasn't around. Probably off licking his wounds. The whip had dug into the stupid man's back, stippled it. Sexto had no great love for Jaime. Jaime was tall and slender as if the blood of the Spaniards ran in his veins. But Jaime was also stupid, the dog turd.

Sexto rubbed the stubble on his second chin.

He would have one of his men fetch him water. This shack was no palace, that was for sure, but it had served him well. He would shave today. He was expecting the Americanos.

They, too, were dog turds. But Sexto needed them. They were supposed to be rounding up all the Chiricahuas and forcing them back to the Fort Apache reservation. Once the big drive was on, they would have many more slaves for him.

"Jose," Sexto called to his right-hand man. "Bring water and a basin. Breakfast."

The other man was slumped in a chair, still not recovered from last night. Sexto aimed a kick in his direction. Jose woke up abruptly.

"Move," Sexto told him. "Wake the others. We have company today."

There were five men in all, including Jaime. Except for Sexto's worthless brother-in-law, they were tough and rugged. Not pretty.

Jose had a searing white scar that extended up beyond his hairline from a knife fight some years back. It gave him a white streak of hair and a drooping eyelid.

It was no wonder Jose was loyal to Sexto. Even the whores back in Sonora shuddered when he crossed their doorstep. He was Sexto's enforcer, and he performed his duties well.

Sexto was proud of his right-hand man's cold-blooded brutality. Now there was a bandido who gave women no corner, who enjoyed keeping them in line.

The only problem with Jose, Sexto thought, was those googly eyes he had given the Americano soldier last time. If Joseph Tibbs got drunk enough today, who knows what Jose would do to him?

Bah!

Sexto spat on the earth floor and bellowed, "*Arriba!* Up, you lazy sons of whores."

CHAPTER NINE

The *chuck-chuck-chuck* of a chuckwalla lizard woke Glidinghawk. The sun was well past its zenith and sinking toward the west. He had slept many hours, but he did not feel refreshed. Hunger and thirst gnawed at him like a rat chewing on his bowels.

When he moved, he felt the hollow emptiness of the flesh that had been burned away. He would have to check his wound. If it was slick with pus, he would roll over and go back to sleep. He would be a dead man by tomorrow morning.

Gingerly, he stripped the bandages, feeling behind him, prodding his fingers along his aching ribs. He felt that the hollow empty spot was crusted over and hard like metal. That was good.

Except it meant he would have to forage.

He had not told the others what the effort had cost him earlier. He had insisted that they take his meager offerings with them. He hoped they had found water.

Now, his only responsibility was to survive.

For what, Glidinghawk could not have said. He no longer had a beast of burden. If he regained his strength, he might yet lose his life walking out through the desert. But he must try.

Glidinghawk examined his hands, and saw that they were swollen from the cactus barbs. Reddish welts had raised there, making it painful to clench his hands into a fist. His fingers would be clumsy.

Way north, where his people lived, it would be almost time for the corn harvest. He thought of the clean, rustling stalks and golden kernels of corn.

Out here, the Navaho Apaches farmed the land for corn, but the grain it bore was dried and small, not large and succulent.

The Chiricahua did not farm. They hunted and foraged for their food. In these times, they raided the spoils of others. Glidinghawk must make himself think like a Chiricahua Apache.

They had dwelled here for hundreds of years, migrating from the cold, snowy regions far further north of where Glidinghawk's people, the Omaha Sioux, lived.

If the Chiricahua could wrest life from this harsh land, so could he, Glidinghawk resolved.

He assessed his situation. He had no horse to secure. The gold Landrum left with him would only be useful in barter with men.

The Remington repeating rifle might save his life, if he came across a cougar or rattlesnake. It also might be used to shoot game, if by stroke of luck a wild burro or desert rabbit should stray his way.

Now, Glidinghawk was sorry that he had left One Whose Spirit Is Set Free to rot in the sun. He could have made strips of horsemeat from the dead horse. By now it was too risky. One who ate tainted meat in the desert died quickly of dehydration. Diarrhea could kill out here.

The burning ball of flame in the sky was sinking further. Glidinghawk heard the rustle of day creatures sensitive to temperature changes settle for the night. Or he thought that is what he heard, the faint rustle of scales and feathers whispering across rock and sand.

Besides the chuckwalla that had wakened him, there were gecko lizards, small horny toads, snakes and birds—eagles, hawks, wrens and vultures, but not the night-flying owl, who would come out later to hoot his mournful warning.

Right now, Glidinghawk saw the vultures that feasted on the putrid flesh of One Whose Spirit Is Set Free crane their balding, ugly necks to one another, like old stoop-shouldered men planning their comfort for the night.

The other creatures, the desert tortoises, scorpions, tarantulas and other insects, had no heat sensors. They would be scurrying through the night. The land that looked so barren was alive with hidden creatures who had adapted to this climate.

Glidinghawk could feel a certain beauty in the twilight as the shadows on the distant mountains deepened to a rich purple color. In full sun, everything was flattened and lacking in contour. In this light, the slight inclines and depressions took on a depth and majesty.

The first barbed sting stopped Glidinghawk's reverie. Yesterday—was it only yesterday?—he had not harvested the large barrel cacti. A man had to be right there, to sip the juice before it spilled into a thirsty earth. That would not have helped Celia and Landrum at all.

But Glidinghawk had been told that once the art of opening the spherical, spiney trunks was mastered, the watery pulp yielded much life-sustaining liquid.

He attacked, steeling himself not to be drawn to the seductive pool of poisoned water nearby. His knife was dulled. It had a stain of brownish dried blood on it. Glidinghawk stared at it for a long time. It bothered him.

As he knelt to rub grains of sand along the blade to clean it, he saw, out of the corner of his eye, a hatch of grubs at the base of the barrel cactus. White, fat, wriggling.

He picked up a handful in his swollen palm and wolfed them down. Their skin burst under his strong teeth, releasing soft, wet sustenance. It was, Glidinghawk knew, all in the mind. These, he tried to think of as desert berries, which they resembled in texture.

Then he slashed the root of the barrel cactus, near where it grew from the ground. He willed himself not to flinch when fresh barbs stung his infected hands.

Thirstily, he knelt down and placed his parched lips against the tantalizing slit. Hands straining to open the cut, he felt the flow reach his mouth and throat. He sucked at the plant, getting a barb directly above his eye. He hardly noticed.

Like an animal, he took several hours to feed himself and replenish the moisture his healing tissues craved. Toward dawn, well satisfied, he slept again.

When he woke, Glidinghawk made a mark in the sand.

He knew it would be easy to lose all track of time, to

sleep and feed and wither away without noticing the changing phases of the moon.

When he had four marks in the sand, he knew he was well and able to travel. In one way, he was sorry to leave his peaceful routine. He had been at one with the earth, the wind, the moon and the sun.

But the cacti had been drained, and he had to travel further to forage. There were no more clutches of eggs or succulent grubs. Things in the desert grew slowly. He would have to move on.

Having strength enough to stay and sleep and eat and suck cactus juice was not the same as having the strength to travel long distances, Glidinghawk knew.

He would have to travel lightly. As it was, he had taken to wearing the dead Apache's breechclout. His skin, already bronze, had turned a deep mahogany. His jet black hair was drawn back from his head by a leather thong.

In looks, he knew he was more savage than any Indian he had come up against, and his time in the wilderness had honed his eyes and ears to every small movement.

Yesterday when the sun was high in the sky, he had alerted to the faint slithering of a huge rattler. He could have used his rifle to kill the serpent, but it seemed out of place, out of keeping.

Instead, he had pinned the huge diamond-back to the ground with the sharp-tipped Apache spear. Later, he had cut large chunks of snake meat and let them dry in the sun until they were tough and brown and hard. They would be food for his journey.

The rest of the flesh, he had chewed, bloody and fresh and dripping down his chin. He felt its strength and cunning running through his blood now.

He tried not to let himself think of Celia or Landrum.

By now, they had made it or they were dead. There was no use in agonizing over their fate. Deep inside, he had the disquieting feeling that they had reached water, but were now in grave danger.

That had come to the solitary Omaha in a dream that was almost a vision. For many years—ever since the missionaries had sent him to the reservation school and, later, to the huge, white man's university— Glidinghawk had tried to quell his dreams.

Heathen superstition, the white men told him.

Once, he had a dream so strong he went to his adoptive mother about it. He remembered her stern look and long-suffering eyes when he told her that the old shaman from his tribe was dying, and he felt that the old man's power was invading his own body. She called her husband, who beat Glidinghawk with a belt. He was told to pray and ask forgiveness.

But the dreams had come back to him, and the wise words of the old shaman. "Some men are born with the gift," the white-haired elder had told him. "If you use and believe it, it will serve you well. You can feel what other men need words to tell them."

In this half-waking, half-sleeping dream, Glidinghawk had seen Celia tied to a post while short, squat, swarthy men laughed and drank deeply of the firewater.

He saw Landrum in a small room, locked in helplessness.

Maybe it was only Glidinghawk's imagination. He had sensed that Landrum was heading for the slaver's camp. He had known that was the choice he would have made.

Strange, that one moment he had been sure they were happy and free—Landrum and Celia, splashing and laughing in a stream whose water was clear and bubbling with life—the next, a dark cloud of evil snatched them up. And now, Glidinghawk could almost see the cruel, laughing faces of their captors.

So, although Glidinghawk had been about to bury the gold Landrum left with him—it was a heavy burden to tote on legs that would have trouble with the long miles ahead—he thought better of it.

When he counted the bullion, Glidinghawk was surprised. There was more than he had imagined. Landrum, apparently, had feared that Surefoot would not be able to bear the weight. So now, the responsibility of $1500 worth of gold was on his shoulders.

As it was, none of them had figured out how the army came up with the figure of $3000. That, Lieutenant Colonel Smith at Fort Lowell told them, was the exact amount they would be given in gold, to use as their cover as slavers. What they didn't know was that the figure was the amount the army had authorized for expenses for the three of them per annum.

And some accountant back in Washington City had figured that if they came back alive, they would be returning it. If not—which was likely in the army's eyes—the budget would not be overdrawn.

Gold . . . a small but heavy package.

Glidinghawk kicked the saddlebags with his foot. If he had any kind of beast he would be a lot more confident. He had hoped, during the last four days, that some wild burros would come clomping his way.

They hadn't.

He was tempted to rest one more day, but a force drew him onward like a magnet. This was the right time to leave his desert nest. Tonight he must travel. He must obey the voice within him that told him to go.

Sorting through his possessions was not difficult. The weapons, including the spear, he would need. His ammunition was low, but he did have bullets left, encased in their brass housing, dry and fully charged.

He made a sack of his buckskin shirt and trousers. He would travel lightly dressed, but they might, later, afford some protection from the sun and other elements.

The dried snake meat he took, and the lobes of cochineal cactus stripped of their barbs. He hoped to happen on more grubs and eggs along the way.

Glidinghawk had always been tall and lean. Now, his bones protruded from beneath his darkened skin. His hipbones jutted out as sharply as his ribs. His stomach, which had never had the rounded softness of the white man, was concave.

He strapped his heavy load on his back. The moon was showing, a sliver of silver peeking through before the sun had set. He had to leave the Apache shield behind, and the saddle. They were too clumsy to carry.

Using the spear as a walking stick, he set out. Due north, the way the others had gone. He hummed a toneless chant to give him courage.

The stars came out, a few brightly winking, the others spilled across the sky in clusters like dewdrops. Glidinghawk felt very small in a universe that was very grand and endless.

He no longer thought of this alien territory as the

enemy. He had become one with it, one with the life force of the land.

If he could only glide with the ebb and flow of this great universe, he knew he would be all right. He felt that so strongly, he was not surprised when toward the dawn, he saw a strange beast ambling across his path, swaying from side to side to like a ship on the desert.

It was half again the height of a tall man and oddly shaped, with a huge humped back. Glidinghawk's mind fished back for what the Apache stablehand had told him about the few weird creatures running wild in the desert.

"They have strong teeth and evil tempers, no good for a man to ride or eat," the Indian had told him.

Well, Glidinghawk would just see about that.

In the white man's language, Glidinghawk was pretty sure he had stumbled upon a camel—unless his senses had left him and he was having hallucinations.

The only problem was, how do you catch a wild camel?

CHAPTER TEN

Landrum had been all for moving on as soon as they filled their canteens and rested, but Celia changed his mind. She was splashing, laughing and drinking in the stream.

Celia was beautiful in the dappled sunlight. Her wet hair gleamed a deep red, hanging in wet tendrils around her face. Joy and relief mingled on her face.

Landrum had joined her. Out of deference, he had taken off his shirt but wore his trousers. Celia's shirt, a man's shirt made of broadcloth, was wet and molded to her body, as were her trousers.

He could tell how thin she had become, as if the last few days had melted the flesh from her. Still, she was slightly rounded in all the right places, and a treat to see. Now that his thirst was slaked, it crossed his mind that it had been a long time since he'd had a woman.

Strange, that a near-brush with death did that to him every time. Made him randier than a bull—something he would do his best to conceal from the woman at his side. She had been through enough.

He cupped his hands and brought water up to his unshaven, dusty face. He drank and washed and did not complain about the mud he was stirring up. After a time, he became curious.

"Hey, Ceil, did you think we'd ever get you out of the Apache camp?"

She became very still and serious, but the mood did not last long. "I had faith in you two," she said simply. "But I was prepared to become an Indian squaw. I'm not sure, but I think those braves had a plan for me — one I wasn't going to like."

"Were they Cochise's band?" Landrum asked.

"The leader I saw was not that old. His name was Naiche. I think he is Cochise's second son."

"The father of Saguaro Flower?"

"Probably. But everything happened so quickly, I am not sure what would have happened. I don't speak the language. There was an old woman who spoke French, a kind of French. She talked to me. She had been the squaw of a trader many moons back, she said."

"What did she tell you?"

"She was afraid. She whispered that I might be traded for the Apache maiden they wanted back. The warriors were fighting with Naiche about it. One of them wanted to claim me for his bride."

"They didn't . . . the brave that took you didn't harm you?" Landrum asked. He was trying to be delicate. What he meant was, were you raped?

Celia shook her head. She splashed Landrum's face and laughed. It was behind her now. She had been terrified. She wanted to forget it.

Landrum splashed back at her, and their play escalated into a full scale water fight. Neither of them was yet strong, but the fresh water had released a reserve of energy that overflowed.

As they frolicked, Landrum was aware that his wet trousers revealed his growing manhood. He saw Celia gaze there, and quickly look away. He retreated to the bank of the stream.

"When you are ready, we should eat," he said. "Hardtack and beef jerky—it sounds like a feast now that we have water."

She joined him. Landrum turned his attention to chewing and swallowing.

"Anything wrong?" Celia asked.

"Just saddle sore—and this damned minie ball in my backside kicks up sometimes. It's nothing," Landrum lied.

It was a golden afternoon. Some mesquite trees grew nearby, after being seeded by the droppings of deer or perhaps mountain sheep. Although it was hot, it was pleasant, with their wet clothing cooling their skin.

Landrum leaned back and cradled his head in hands crossed behind his neck. He stared up at the cloudless blue sky. He saw wisps of smoke rising into the air like angry exclamation points.

Celia leaned her head back, also. Her face was flushed from the sun. Her head wound was healing nicely. She had washed it and it showed no sign of infection. He reached out and touched her cheek, quietly getting her attention.

"Yes?" she said lazily. She looked peaceful and content. Landrum hated to alarm her.

"I see smoke," he said quietly. "I'm afraid we might have company. Sexto Diaz's camp should be located around here, unless I am mistaken. I think we should hide, and head west in the morning, before full sun."

At first, Landrum thought she was agreeing, but

then her eyes blanked out. "I want to play," she whined.

Before he could stop her, she had stripped off her shirt and run down to the water where, like a child, she sat and splashed.

"Celia, put your clothes on," he called softly.

"I won't."

Landrum's breath rasped in his throat. She was so gorgeous and frail he felt stabbed by her beauty and vulnerability, as if he had been struck by Cupid's arrow.

But he also knew he couldn't take advantage of her.

She was not herself. Further, she was making too much noise. That smoke meant fire, and men. Sounds echoed through the hills.

Landrum wondered how long it would be before Celia's mind stayed on a single plane, instead of darting back and forth between the here and now and another time and place long ago. He hoped she would soon recover; there was just so much a man could take.

He strode down to where she lay on her back.

"Come on, Celia," he said, more sharply than he had intended. "We need to hide."

He reached down and lifted her into his arms. She kicked and bit his hand, then settled back and placed her wet head against his shoulder. That was when a glint of metal attracted him to the hill on the other side of the gorge. It flashed briefly, but the sparkle hurt his eyes.

Landrum put Celia down and reached for her shirt. "Put this on," he said. He took his rifle and aimed it across the way. He was sure he had seen company — unwelcome company. The only good thing was that his lust was now firmly under control. Dammit.

But now, he saw nothing to shoot at.

He saw that Celia was fully clad. "I think we have trouble," he said tensely. "Are you . . . yourself now?"

She nodded. "Yes, but my head aches and—oh Landrum, I am sorry. I don't know what I was doing."

He patted her shoulder. Clumsy and not too comforting, but it was the best he could do. He was not about to hug her to him and tell her it would be all right. His feelings were just below the surface ready to rise again—along with another thing that was giving him trouble.

When I hit the next town, Landrum promised himself, *I'm going to find me a red-headed whore and do it until I drop.*

Then he chuckled. It broke the sexual tension.

But he had a heap of other things to figure out, besides cooling his own fires. He put a brotherly—well, he tried to make it brotherly—arm around Celia's shoulder and led her back to where Surefoot was dozing.

"I thought our best bet was to ride on, but you aren't well yet and I'm pretty certain that was trouble I spotted in those hills. Let's hope if we don't walk right into it, it won't come to us."

"What do we do?" Celia asked.

The party was over. Their thirst had been satisfied. They had eaten. Splashing and reveling in the mountain stream no longer held much appeal, only danger.

"About five feet back yonder, I see a likely spot, in the rocks there"—he pointed to a cave-like hollow. "I'm going to check it out. Maybe we can hide there, tie the horse nearby."

Celia waited while he made preparations.

Landrum tried the crawl space and found it roomy

enough for them to lie in. He laid buckskin over the natural earthen floor. Surefoot was more of a problem—that, and the fact that droppings suggested that this had once been some animal's lair. Still, maybe the mountain cat, or whatever it was, was long gone. They would have to chance it.

Landrum went to get Celia.

All of a sudden, he saw her doubling over. Landrum could tell she felt a rumbling from deep in her stomach. He had cautioned her not to overdo it, but any water and food after the last few days was a lot.

Immediately, Landrum realized he was experiencing the same rumblings himself. Gas. His belly felt swelled out worse than a pregnant pig's.

Green-faced and miserable, he helped Celia walk back to the relative safety of the cold camp. It was hidden from plain view by the outcropping of rock along the gorge.

They settled down to suffer out the next few hours until nightfall. Celia was all right some of the time. At others, she whimpered and cried.

When darkness came, they slept.

Landrum kept waking up wondering if that glint he had seen was a rifle barrel. Celia woke up, too. They both turned at the same time and bumped heads.

"Sorry," Landrum said.

"Sorry," Celia said.

They were lying face to face in the enclosure. The top of Celia's head came to rest on Landrum's chest. Her fine hair tickled his nose.

"I have to go outside," Celia whispered.

"Me, too," Landrum admitted. "We'd better go together—and stick pretty close together."

They crawled out. Surefoot nickered at them and quieted immediately. The phase of the moon had changed; it was no longer full.

Nights out here were never pitch black. There were rarely any clouds. That's why Landrum assumed the wispy gray floating across the face of the moon was smoke from a campfire. It never occurred to him it was the slight hint of rain clouds forming.

This was the end of July—or maybe already August. Landrum had lost track of the dates. The sun hugged the earth now, shortly before it reached its autumn equinox, making the days longer and the nights brighter.

Bright enough so night did not guarantee modesty.

Celia looked around her uncertainly. There were no clumps of bushes or hiding spots. Landrum saw the same thing. The last thing he wanted to do was prowl around too far from safety.

He placed a strong hand on Celia's shoulder and said, "You point yourself in the direction of the Big Dipper, I'll walk about ten paces away and face south. Give a shout when you're finished."

"And I wonder what Miss Parsons' Finishing School for Young Ladies would say to that," Celia said lightly.

But she was quick to follow his suggestion. The situation was becoming desperate. She was mortified by the sounds coming from her body, but she could hear Landrum was going through the same agony.

Squatting and miserable, she did not notice the moon shut out by the clouds, either. In the desert, rain is an unusual and exotic experience. It only happens at certain times of the year.

Rainfall in these arid areas was only about 12 inches

a year. There was no reason for either Celia or Landrum to expect it. Glidinghawk had heard of it — had heard enough to fear a deluge almost as much as the constant drought.

True, most non-desert areas had 200 inches of rain or more a year. The pittance the Arizona Territory received from an ungenerous benefactor was nothing.

The trouble was, when rain came to these parched lands, it came all at once. The hard, crusty earth could not absorb it. It swept a watery death in its path.

But that was the last thing on Landrum's mind.

"Are you through?" he called.

Celia answered softly. She felt better, but embarrassed. She envied men, being so free and open and never blushing. She managed to get along in a man's world, but at times like these the effort was a strain.

Together, they went back to their cave.

At this hour, a chill stillness had settled in, and they did not suffer too much from the lack of breeze. Landrum's long, lean body sprawled out beside Celia's.

He felt very close to her, but his stomach problems had effectively quelled his lust. It was different, having Celia around.

All his life, Landrum had thought that women were creatures far removed from the rough-and-tumble world of men.

Sure, his own mother and grandmother had been the kind they call the salt of the earth. They were pioneers, used to enduring hardship and standing by their men.

But they also went to church and prayed a lot and insisted on their modesty.

Then, in the scheme of things, there were the loose

women, who did not go to church and who did not pray. They, Landrum knew, had a different kind of toughness under their finery.

Celia was different from any of them, he thought as he tried to drift off to sleep. Even after sharing the rigors of the trail with her—rigors that put them on an equal footing—he wanted her.

Knowing that she was not a virgin did not make her a fallen woman, in his eyes. Yes, she was something entirely different in his experience.

Several times now, Celia had saved his life.

That first time, back in Abilene, when she had whipped out that silly derringer of hers and shot the man who was after Glidinghawk, Landrum flat out didn't know what to make of her.

Even now, he had an inward chuckle thinking of how pretty and feminine she looked for a woman who had a gun tucked in her garter and knew how to use it.

Ever since, Celia had been surprising him.

Today, when she risked her life—or at least her well-formed limbs—to get Surefoot back on the mountainous trail, she had been braver and more sensible than many men he had traveled with.

In fact, thinking back on his career, first as an officer in the Confederate Army, then as a Texas Ranger, he could not recall any of the people he worked with whom he would rather have by his side than Glidinghawk and Celia.

We're all mavericks, he thought, *and Celia isn't like any woman I ever met—or ever will. She's a lady and a brother and a teammate all rolled into one. And I'd better stop thinking about her before I get in trouble with that damned club between my legs again.*

His eyelids growing heavy, Landrum was very much aware of Celia turning to him and instinctively molding herself into his prone body.

Sleepily, Landrum marveled that the man who hired him, Lt. Col. Amos Powell back at the Territorial Command in Fort Leavenworth, Kansas, had possessed the wisdom to insist on a woman as a member of the team.

He also wondered if Powell had any idea how hard it made it on a man sometimes.

Celia was a nuisance and it wasn't because she was lily-livered or weak. It was because he felt the overwhelming desire to protect her and that wasn't always easy.

Landrum was almost asleep, but the smoke and the glint of metal he had seen today had him worried. His mind rolled around before getting comfortable.

He figured that that priggish Second Lt. Preston Kirkwood Fox should be somewhere in the area by now, acting as an inspector for the US Army.

What that meant exactly Landrum did not know, except the little pantywaist should have some freedom to move around. Maybe the man could get them out of this one.

When it was a choice between dying and walking right into the enemy camp, Landrum had thought, fine, we'll go ahead and take it from there.

Now, he wanted to get away from the bandeleros who roamed these hills. Mexicans could be tough and cruel, and they had no more liking for Americanos than they had for Apache slaves.

Besides, Glidinghawk was never far from Landrum's thoughts. Landrum had the gut feeling that the Indian had survived, but he was stuck out there in the middle of nowhere.

So the best thing to do was get help, travel back to that poisoned oasis and mesa and get Glidinghawk out. Then the three of them would be together again — Powell's Army.

Their mission was crucial, Landrum knew.

Powell wasn't a bad man or a foolish one. He would not have sent them to this hellhole unless it was pretty damned important.

Landrum sighed.

All this thinking was interfering with his sleeping time. Besides, if he slept, he might dream about having a woman. Celia.

It didn't hurt anything to dream, did it?

CHAPTER ELEVEN

Captain Honorius Crawford of the Fort Apache garrison was getting drunk with Sexto Diaz. On the surface, the captain was typical officer material—he cleaned under his fingernails, wore his uniform jacket in summer, and had his mutton chops trimmed by the sutler on a regular basis. He had a side deal going there. His trims were free.

Now his blue uniform jacket was tossed aside. His shirt was opened at the collar, showing more hairy, sagging belly than masculine breadth of chest. Sweat ringed his armpits and his slate gray eyes blurred from alcohol.

His thoughts, too, reverted to the vulgar—something he had careful control over back at the garrison. And why not, when he was dealing with a rough bunch of slobs?

That, Honorius knew, included Master Sergeant Joseph Tibbs, his partner in crime. Secretly, Honorius Crawford had great contempt for the shanty Irishman who had risen through the army ranks. But Tibbs had been his salvation.

The captain and Tibbs had ridden to Sexto's mountain hideaway to make plans for the next shipment of Chiricahuan slaves. Another year of roundups—Honorius did not think of Indians as people so much as cantankerous cattle with a certain value per head—and he would retire.

Unlike the embezzlement scheme he had been involved in back in Philadelphia, this was working. No one had found out about that one, but it had driven Honorius west.

The army, Captain Crawford knew, would take anyone.

And the army, finally, with a little finagling on his part, was doing all right for Crawford. The way he figured it, he was doing the army a favor and getting something on the side for himself. They needed to get rid of Indians for the westward expansion. He was helping them, right?

He was in his mid-thirties and feeling it. His spreading gut and thinning sandy hair told him it was about time to get rich and retire. Back East. And at the rate he was going, capturing and selling Apaches, he just might be able to. Another year . . .

After all, why would a man want to risk his life fighting redmen when he could make them into slaves instead? Honorius didn't much like army discipline or orders, but he was crafty. He put up with it and bided his time. He had a good army record.

When they had ordered him to round up the Chiricahua and get their red asses to the reservation, he had smelled his chance.

Joseph Tibbs had been the one to come up with this scheme—and why not, for a quarter of what they made? The burly master sergeant was fat and stupid—

at least in Honorius' estimation—but he could rattle off that Spanish lingo and get along with the bandeleros.

Privately, Honorius believed it was because Tibbs had that scuffling peasant mentality himself.

When the two soldiers arrived at the bandeleros' camp, Sexto's men Santos and Manuel were out guarding the westward mountain pass. Or that's what they were supposed to be doing.

Honorius had caught them sleeping on the job, sombreros pulled down over their faces, rifles lying useless nearby.

Honorius was spitting mad. He looked over his shoulder often and worried about his own security. "I will report this to your boss man," he threatened.

"It is none of your business, long nose," the one named Santos mumbled.

"What did he say?" Crawford asked Tibbs. His own Spanish was serviceable but slow.

"He said he would not let it happen again," Tibbs said. Then, to the guards, he added in gunfire-rapid Spanish, "We will soon get rich and kill this meddling son of a dog, eh? Then we will all take siestas every day."

Manuel and Santos laughed.

They liked Tibbs but hated the other one. They would be glad when they no longer needed the American captain. It would be a pleasure to kill him. More than once, words from Crawford had brought Sexto's whip down upon them.

As the uniformed men rode on, Santos and Manuel promised themselves revenge. Revenge was sweet, but they would never dare take it out on Sexto. He was part of life they had to put up with; the American long nose was not.

Crawford forgot the incident. He took his superiority for granted. The Mexicans catered to him, he thought.

At the camp shack, Sexto had one of his men serve up some burned meat rolled up on a flat bread made of mesa, a flour ground from corn—it tasted worse than Indian food looked, almost made a man grateful for army food.

The whole mess had been spiced with chili peppers that would burn the lining right out of a man's stomach. Sexto didn't seem too happy with the meal, either, or maybe it was that man Jaime who had cooked it.

Honorius wondered if Jaime was being punished by the kitchen detail. Certainly, he had recently been punished in other ways; the welts on his back weren't from good conduct.

Awful stuff, that Mex food, but it was washed down with tequila. Powerful but raw, it made a man feel good deep down inside—but not as good as the thought of all the money they were making.

Only a man like myself, Honorius thought, *could pull this off*.

Sexto belched loudly. "How soon can you bring me more squaws?"

He spoke to Crawford, but loudly enough so Tibbs could hear. Sexto knew that Crawford thought of himself as the numero uno, the big boss man, the mastermind. For now, Sexto was willing to go along with that charade.

"Maybe next week," Honorius said. "We are supposed to be rounding up stray bands in a few days.

Some of them just might not make it to the reservation, if you know what I mean. There might be a holdup, though. Tibbs will explain it to you."

Sexto winked broadly at the rotund master sergeant. *Madre de Dios*, Sexto thought, *the captain's Spanish is bad*.

Tibbs took over. He told Sexto about the new army man, a tinhorn named Fox, who was surveying the situation out here. Tibbs rat-a-tatted the lingo so fast Honorius did not get the gist of his entire conversation.

Tibbs said that they could always kill this Fox if he came snooping around, and no one would be the wiser. Sexto nodded in agreement. He did not mind killing Americanos.

"I want more money up front this time," the captain said, a look of greed stealing into his eyes, to go along with the sly smile across his face.

Sexto poured another shot of tequila. He pretended not to hear. Honorius slugged his back and waited. He hated dealing with this fat, greasy tub of lard. But they had made a gentleman's agreement.

Neither, of course, was a gentleman, but Captain Honorius had delusions. Honor among thieves was one of his favorite sayings. The men who had ended up in jail back in Philadelphia would have disagreed with him.

"Well?" Honorius finally asked. He twirled a fat, Mexican cigar in his hands. Their smokes were far better than their atrocious food.

"Que?" Sexto replied, toying with the officer. He planned to raise the ante a little, since he had gotten top peso for the virgin, but he liked making the army man sweat.

"You explain it to him!" Honorius told Tibbs in

English. "You're on their level. Pesos. Money. Extra for top merchandise."

Joseph was getting drunk, but he saw what the game was and he sided with Sexto. Make the captain grovel, it was no skin off his back. He was enjoying himself.

Besides, he had a side deal with the Mexican slaver—one that the captain did not know about.

Honorius Crawford would be thrown a bone, but Tibbs was getting the meat. Tibbs planned to do away with the captain after this next shipment and hightail it to Mexico. A man could live well down there, and he liked the women.

Besides, having that Second Lieutenant Fox snooping around on behalf of the army told him the game would soon be over. Add to that the chance a man took getting killed by these Apache savages, and south of the border began to look better.

A smart man, Tibbs thought, *knows when to fold his hand—and Crawford is too greedy to be smart.*

"I was talking money," Honorius repeated, surly. "Tell him we want $1,000 today."

Sexto knew some English. He understood dollar talk. His face flushed a deep purple. Tibbs was right, this Americano was getting too big for his britches. It would be a pleasure to kill him after the biggest roundup of all.

Using Tibbs as an interpreter, Sexto said, "Ah, we will throw him $500 today, for his expenses. In return, we want at least fifty Indians, most of them women. A few children, if they are strong, I can sell. But mostly women. Tell him there will be a bonus when he delivers—and you and I know what his bonus will be. Blam!"

The swarthy slaver laughed loudly at his own wit. Tibbs nodded. Yes, better to placate Honorius with gold now than have him grumbling. Better that the captain enthusiastically got more bodies on this next roundup. Blinded by gold, Crawford would not suspect it would be his last.

"$500," he told Honorius.

In English, mumbling to Tibbs, the captain beamed. "Didn't I tell you that he would offer half of what I asked? I know how to work these peasants. Tell him $900."

The haggling continued. Honorius' eyes widened when he was told how many Indians he needed to supply. But he was drunk. He was more tuned into the money angle than the staggering number of captives.

The up-front money was finally settled at a figure of $750. In return, the captain promised delivery within the week. Over the captain's slumped shoulders, Sexto winked at Tibbs. The men drank.

The bottle was finished.

Sexto crashed it to the floor. It exploded into a million shards of glass. He called for more libation. Jaime served them. Sexto aimed a kick in his direction.

The handsome Mexican with Spanish blood in his veins narrowed his eyes and thought of the intruders in the hills. He hoped Manuel and Santos were too lazy to spot them. He hoped that they were enemies of Sexto Diaz.

Jose joined the group. The white stripe on his head and his ugly scar made Honorius uncomfortable. Worse, the man's eyes glittered madly when he looked at the Americanos.

After a while, they no longer pretended to talk

business. The talk turned to women. Jaime saw that they were well supplied, and slipped away.

He walked away from camp on quiet feet. This was no life for a man, he thought. He had been with Sexto three years now, since the swarthy bandido had married his sister Carmen. Carmen, like himself, was tall, lithe, and had the fire of Spain in her dancing eyes.

Nothing about Carmen Diaz danced any more. Her eyes had lost their sparkle. She was not so much married to Sexto as in bondage to him.

Carmen had been forced to marry the squat, uncouth bandido leader over a bad family debt. Jaime had been taken in as one of Sexto's men—more to keep Carmen in line when Sexto was away than anything else.

It was not a happy life for Jaime or for his sister.

Jaime was a coward. He would never dare kill the Mexican slaver himself. But he prayed nightly that someone else would come along and do it for him.

Then, Jaime thought, he and his sister would be free.

Jaime edged down to the gorge. He saw the clouds billow across the quartered face of the moon. At first, he had hated the country out here, and longed for the stucco houses and cantinas of home.

But away from the shack and the corrals—corrals built to hold human flesh rather than horse flesh—he had found peace. Moments of peace in which he prayed and renewed himself.

The creek was one of his spots.

Across the way, he was sure he heard human voices. Not the gruff voices of soldiers or rival bandits. A woman's voice is difficult to mistake, even when it whispers Anglo words.

Jaime also saw dark forms squatting in the rocks, not far from where the magnificent wildcat reigned.

Whoever it was had taken refuge in the cougar's cave. That's what Jaime called it, though it was only a crevice in the rocks on the other side of the gorge.

He had an understanding with the cougar who used to live there. Jaime had watched the beast, muscles rippling, pace the cliffs. The huge cat was another thing Jaime had never reported. One of the men would have hunted it.

Instead, Jaime had hoped that one drunken night, the cougar would find Sexto. Now the cougar was gone, but humans had taken its place.

Maybe they would get Sexto.

Maybe on the next trip south to Sonora, Sexto would meet with an accident.

Maybe the soldiers—the ones back at the fort, not the scum who dealt with Sexto—would finally catch up to the greasy slaver.

Jaime took out his rosary beads and began to pray.

The next day, he wondered if God had been listening. With Jose's help, Sexto captured Landrum and Celia before they could put up a fight.

CHAPTER TWELVE

"Become as one with the animal you are hunting," the old shaman had once told Glidinghawk. "Walk as he walks, talk as he talks and think as he thinks, and you can capture him. He who stalks his brother is the most deadly hunter, because he knows his brother deep inside. Let your spirit become brother to the animal you wish to subdue, and you will be a mighty hunter."

All that was terrific advice, Glidinghawk thought, but what the hell did he know about camels?

They were ugly, mean-tempered creatures who traveled the desert regions of the world. Well, Glidinghawk felt about the same way himself, right now. But he doubted that would help him catch the camel.

He paused as the high-humped beast came to within fifty yards, sniffling with curiosity.

Were camels dumb? Glidinghawk wondered. He might as well work on that assumption, because if this rat-haired creature was smart, Glidinghawk didn't stand a chance.

The camel stopped and stared.

Big eyes, a nose that looked like that of a mutant

horse, and lips that drew back in a sneer. The expression across that camel's face was almost human—and like that of no man Glidinghawk would care to associate with.

Cunning but dumb, Glidinghawk decided. But how skittish? The Indian raised a hand and the animal bolted back three paces, still curious but cautious.

Funny looking creature, with that mound on his back, skinny neck and thin, long legs. A fast traveler, Glidinghawk knew from watching the beast heave forward through the night.

Glidinghawk was walking with the pack on his back. There was no way he could make himself look like a camel.

Or was there?

Not a tall camel, anyway. Maybe a camel on his knees or resting on his belly, though. Glidinghawk sized up his chances. Between slim and none. He didn't have anything to lose by trying a few Indian tricks.

Look as he looks?

Glidinghawk slid down on his hands and knees and arched his back so that his backpack made a solid hump. At least his pose was not threatening to the camel, who edged a little closer.

Glidinghawk saw that it was a male camel. He wondered if that made any difference. With horses, mares were generally more docile and easily led. But with Arab mounts?

Having graduated from the university, Glidinghawk had studied geography. Dartmouth was like so many of the eastern schools, teaching European and British perspective rather than delving into the raw land of the west.

Sometimes, listening to the academics, Glidinghawk had wondered if they had ever truly broken from England.

However, learning about the massive British Empire also meant learning about the Arab territories—and they were big on camels.

Then, too, Glidinghawk was aware of the American experiment, long since abandoned, of bringing camels to the southwestern United States. Landrum had talked about it.

This beast, he surmised, was one of a small band that had run wild after the experiment had been given up. He had probably never been tamed. But perhaps, like a wild mustang, he could be brought under control and used.

Camels . . . Glidinghawk wracked his brains trying to think. It was no use. He could not remember any lore that would be useful to him. He would have to look and listen to the living example in front of him and do his best.

The camel snickered at him—not like a horse, but like an old man spitting tobacco juice when he snorted out a joke.

Glidinghawk made a guttural, spitting sound deep in his throat, halfway between a juice-spitting hawk and a chuckle. It got the camel's attention.

The beast made another sound, rather an obscene bellow.

Glidinghawk wriggled his mock hump and replied in kind.

The camel came closer. The animal's nostrils quivered. Glidinghawk knew that the scent was of the dead fish. It still clung to the leather pouch they had been carried in.

Amazed, Glidinghawk watched the camel lower his head and step into range. Glidinghawk tensed his muscles. He would not have more than one chance to capture this camel, he knew.

If the beast spooked, that would be the end. There was no way Glidinghawk could pursue him on foot. So he snort-snickered and tried to look camel-like.

If he comes close, I will throw my arms around his neck and hold on, Glidinghawk thought. He had done that many times catching horses. He had a lasso ready.

Glidinghawk had done his best to look like the camel, to talk like him. The real difficult part was to think like him. Did the beast, under his fear, want company?

Glidinghawk had been alone in the wilderness for four days. He was at peace with it, but the sight of another living thing made his heart glad.

Maybe the camel felt the same way.

Certainly, the wandering beast was willing to take a chance on this stranger—as long as Glidinghawk stayed fairly still and played camel.

Glidinghawk forced himself to breathe slowly and normally. The camel was almost within spitting distance. Glidinghawk smelled the bad breath wafting from the animal's mouth. It was almost enough to knock him over backward.

That mouth, on closer inspection, was less attractive than Glidinghawk had realized. The camel's big teeth were yellowed and spaced far apart. The sneer did nothing to further Glidinghawk's confidence.

The camel nuzzled his open, sneering mouth toward

Glidinghawk's pack. Its strong teeth bit down on the leather. Glidinghawk was pushed to the ground.

He twirled around and lunged.

He threw the rope and wrapped his arms around the camel's neck.

The camel snorted and kicked. Glidinghawk held on. His foot was trampled, but he held his grip.

The beast tossed his head from side to side, threatening with those awesome teeth. A bite sank into Glidinghawk's shoulder. Glidinghawk cursed and tightened his grip.

They struggled. It seemed like a long time to Glidinghawk. The camel was strong. Glidinghawk got bitten twice and his toes were smashed until he picked his lower body off the ground, making the camel drag his full weight.

Man and beast careened across the desert hardpan, fighting and cursing and spitting. Damn, Glidinghawk was being dragged back the way he had come, back toward the mesa.

One thing about a ride like this, he thought, *is that you can't stop.* Glidinghawk knew he had expended too much precious energy to give up on the camel now.

How many miles they traveled Glidinghawk was not sure. Their direction changed many times. Glidinghawk had slipped a noose over the camel's ridiculously skinny neck. That action had been a miracle.

Clinging to the moving beast was almost impossible. But Glidinghawk had no choice. He thought his arms were going to pull right out of their sockets.

He sensed the camel tiring. He hoped it was tiring. Another minute, and he was ready to roll over and die, himself.

Finally, the beast slowed to a halt, planted its back end firmly on the ground, and turned his head to spit in Glidinghawk's face. The beast refused to budge.

Now it came back to Glidinghawk. Camels were supposed to be the most stubborn animals on earth. Well, two could play that game. This gave Glidinghawk a chance to fasten a bridle of sorts around the camel's mouth, the way he would have done with a horse he wanted to break.

Only wild mustangs did not have the biting power.

Glidinghawk's third finger was bitten almost to the bone by the time he was through. He made the improvised reins very long—just in case he tumbled off and had to hold on to his prize.

Prize? Glidinghawk had rarely smelled anything as bad as this camel. The odor made an old drunk seem perfumed. The matted hair covering the animal was coarse, bristly and stinking.

That fetid breath was worse than a rotting corpse. Glidinghawk's stomach tightened into a hard, rebellious knot of disgust.

But he had a beast of burden.

Once the camel was roped and bridled, Glidinghawk held iron-fisted to the rope and circled forward to look the animal in the eye. Two baleful brown eyes stared back at him.

Glidinghawk had caught and tamed wild animals before. It had never been easy. This was new to him, but he thought he detected a glint of submission in the camel's face.

"I will call you Ship of the Desert," Glidinghawk said.

The camel spit a stream of saliva almost directly into Glidinghawk's mouth. The Indian spit and wiped it away with his arm.

"Beast?" Glidinghawk asked.

The camel snorted.

"Mighty Hump?"

The camel sniggered and lowered its face modestly.

"Okay, Mighty Hump," Glidinghawk said, talking softly the way he had learned as a boy, "we will be friends. We will ride together for a while, and then I will set you free."

The animal, of course, did not understand. It did not want to budge. Glidinghawk felt like a fool, but somehow, it seemed that what he learned from the shaman and his Indian boyhood was all that stood between him and death out here.

Finally, he pushed the camel's rump while singing an encouraging song. The beast rose and kicked him in the shin. Glidinghawk vaulted to the camel's back and clung to its neck. They lurched onward.

Camels, Glidinghawk was learning, did not buck. They found other ways to make a man uncomfortable. Every time the camel swayed, it seemed to be deliberately crushing the manhood between Glidinghawk's legs.

Still, Glidinghawk and the camel were moving swiftly, and settled into an uneasy truce.

They had a few more battles, about which direction to ride in, but Glidinghawk managed to keep them going north. He estimated their speed at about seven miles an hour. It was, Glidinghawk knew, a miracle.

The sun was not yet high in the sky by the time they reached the Gila foothills. Although Glidinghawk did not know it, he was traveling on a path far west of the one Landrum and Celia had taken. And it was taking him closer to where Manuel and Santos guarded the slaver's hideaway. Glidinghawk knew he was doing well to make progress, to eat up the miles. Later, he thought, he could finesse his direction.

The trouble was, Glidinghawk and the camel kept going higher and higher. Sexto's camp, where Glidinghawk's intuition or psychic powers told him he would find Landrum and Celia, was east-northeast.

Soon, in order to reach them, Glidinghawk would have to head back east, to make up for the west-northwest swing. And the only way to do that would be to go through the guarded mountain pass.

For the moment, though, Glidinghawk was not worried about later. He and Mighty Hump came upon a thin trickle of water that oozed up from an underground spring.

One thing camels were good at, Glidinghawk guessed, was smelling water. Mighty Hump started on his course about two miles away and raced to the finish line.

Glidinghawk had never seen anything as beautiful as the two cottonwood trees bowed over the small patch of water. Except maybe the water itself, a light green liquid that slid down his parched throat like manna from heaven.

The camel, too, drank deeply.

Glidinghawk had never seen any man or beast drink like that. Those curled lips formed a greedy circle and sucked up gallons and gallons of the precious liquid. Mighty Hump did not come up for air.

It was a long time before either of them was sated.

When they were, Glidinghawk tied the beast to a tree and slept. He had come through the desert. The worst, he hoped, was behind him.

He had a sneaking suspicion that the camel beside him was not his friend, the way a horse might be, but the beast was an ally of sorts, a respected adversary.

At least Glidinghawk respected the camel — except for the smell.

"*Soy baracho!*" Santos declared. "I must be drunk. I think I see a big humped beast and a savage. Manuel — heh, Manuel, do you see what I see?"

Manuel halted his pony and stared. "*Si*. Maybe I am drunk, too. I see them. Ah, that Indian looks like a mean one. See, he has a rifle. Never have I seen such a wild looking man. How can it be, from the desert, with a beast like none I have ever seen?"

"Do we run them off with our guns?" Santos asked fearfully.

"Ah, that is foolish, my friend. Who knows what one so savage will do. What if that beast attacks us? I think we will keep this to ourselves. If we tell Sexto, I can feel his whip upon us." Manuel was being judicious.

"Yes," Santos agreed. "Besides, we are supposed to be waiting for the soldiers and their slaves. What harm can one Indian do?"

"A lot," Manuel said glumly. "We go to Sexto with this story, he will know we have been drinking his tequila all day long. Besides, he is too busy with those Americano prisoners."

"*Si*. Such a beauty, the red-headed woman. Not as round as a Mexican, true, but with fire! What would Sexto want with a story, now that he has such a one to humble."

"True. That Jaime, he is looking at that woman like she is the Virgin herself."

"Hah! If she is, Sexto will get extra pesos for her, no? There are buyers who like that white skin and lean meat, eh?"

"*Si*, she is a prize for sure, but what use is a grown man, an Americano? One cannot sell a man."

"Perhaps Jose will take care of him, when he shoots the Americano captain, heh?"

"Too much thought, my friend. Later, when the many Apache maidens come with Tibbs and the one who will be killed, we will have much work."

"That is true. Perhaps today we should drink."

CHAPTER THIRTEEN

Joseph Tibbs was nervous.

Captain Honorius Crawford was in a foul mood, as if he suspected that trouble followed him like the gathering clouds. The fifty-five prisoners, mostly women but some children of both sexes, were being herded east to the Gila Mountain Pass.

Both soldiers had their whips and firearms out in plain view. Joseph's whip cracked as a child ran out of the staggering line of captured Apaches and tried to make for freedom.

The child was a boy of ten, but small. He did not cry. He rejoined his mother's sister in the line of captives. The boy's name was Tortoise, for the Chiricahuan tribe he came from thought he was very slow.

He dreamed of becoming a swift brave someday. Now, since the soldiers flooded into his band's camp and herded him along with the squaws, taking him from his father Brave Eagle, he might never have his chance.

It all happened so quickly. His mother had been

knocked on the head with the butt end of a soldier's rifle and left to die. Perhaps the medicine man would work his magic, and she would live. Either way, his mother was better off than her sister and the others.

Tortoise spoke little—one reason the elders thought he was backward. But he watched and listened. He had known that his band was doing something that was suddenly wrong. He knew that the Great White Father wanted all his brothers and sisters to live up in a barren patch of land.

His father Brave Eagle was among those who rebelled. "We shall live and hunt as we always have. Free."

Tortoise had seen the might of the white soldiers' rifles. He had heard the stories of their deeds. He had been afraid.

He thought, with the reasoning of his ten-year-old mind, that his father and the others should stick their heads in their shells and live where the soldiers told them to live. He did not want to be killed.

But now, this was worse than having age-old hunting grounds taken away. This was living death. There were many soldiers with many guns. They had come to the camp in the dark. Tortoise knew that bad spirits roamed in the dark.

The braves and warriors had been herded in one direction, to the reservation. The young women with bodies that bent like reeds, and breasts as ripe and full as the pitahaya apples were herded in another direction.

The young Apache knew what that meant.

Slavery.

For many years, the Mexicans had raided Apache camps, and the Paiutes. Tortoise had not known that soldiers, too, sought captives to serve them.

The roundup was bloody. Some of the warriors fought, but in the end the braves and the elders, both men and women, had been taken in the direction of the Fort Apache Reservation. The women and children were marched many miles to the east, where the sun rose in the sky.

Other prisoners joined them. Other bands had been raided. It was a black day for all Apaches, not just Tortoise's Chiricahuan band.

It was too bad that all Apaches did not settle their differences, so they could have more might than the white soldiers. There was one old chief Tortoise had heard stories of, the great Cochise. The chief, they said, gathered different Apaches together like brothers to fight the soldiers.

Tortoise wondered if Cochise knew of what was happening here in the wilderness. If only he was not so little and slow, he would tell the old chief. He would get help for his people. For once, Tortoise vowed he would not stick his head back in his shell, deaf and dumb to what was happening around him. He would act.

So, although he did not think he could get away from the fat one with a whip, he darted to the right, away from the staggering line of subdued women and children. Darting would not work. He thought of how a tortoise might slip slowly away. Later he would try again.

* * *

"Maybe we should stop and water them," Tibbs said.

Crawford took a long pull from his canteen. Jose was riding with them also, bringing up the rear. "No. They can go another couple of hours," the captain decided. "I don't like crossing all this territory. I want them out of sight as soon as possible."

Tibbs could not resist the dig. "You think Army Inspector Fox is on your tail?" he sneered.

"The likes of you get court-martialed every day," Honorius said pompously. "I want to keep my record clean."

"So kill the man!" Tibbs exploded.

"Stupid!" Honorius exclaimed. "A man sent from the territorial command gets killed and the army will be all over us. It is not that simple—which you would know if you had any brains. The only thing is, I think the second lieutenant doesn't know his backside from a barn door—as those of your ilk would say."

Tibbs took the insult in stride. After all, he would get his back soon. He didn't like the way they were hurrying the merchandise, though. Some of them could weaken and die.

He was anxious to reach Sexto's camp. A flood of expectation rose in him. Money and retirement—the dishonorable way. But he would care little about his record as a deserter and mountebank when he was safely down in Sonora leading the good life.

Tibbs looked over the batch of slaves. Over forty women to choose from—and he might just hold on to one for his own needs. These Indians squaws had strong backs and legs on them. He just might pick one . . .

Which was precisely what Sexto's chief henchman, Jose, was thinking. Why they had to fill out the body count with children was beyond him—except some of the youngsters had run after their mothers and aunts in the panic of roundup.

Maybe the extra count would mean an added bonus for him, Jose thought. Some of the women were not exactly what he lusted after, but they certainly had nobody to go screaming to when he beat them and took them by force.

He singled one out of the line, saw the way her breasts were so full they strained against her buckskin dress, the way her haunches rolled from side to side as she walked. For a squaw, she wasn't bad. Unless Sexto got her first, Jose would not mind having a go at her.

But Jose was here to keep an eye on the long nosed captain and the other one, the fat master sergeant. What a pair. It was obvious they disliked one another, but they were both so greedy they had fallen in together.

The shorter, burlier one, Tibbs, thought he was going to clean up on the money and leave Crawford with a bullet for his trouble. Jose knew better.

Once the slaves were delivered, they would let Tibbs kill Crawford, Sexto had decided. Tibbs would be useful in herding the human cargo down south.

Then Jose would be allowed to kill Tibbs.

And to sweeten the pot, Jose had been promised a share of the fat master sergeant's money. The future looked rosy indeed.

Almost rosy enough to make up for the irritation of these women caterwauling as they trudged along. Jose snapped his bullwhip. The last woman in line clutched her infant tighter to her breast and stepped more lively.

A baby. They would see about that. If the child started crying, Jose would dispose of the heathen bastard. Had the squaw been a little uglier, he would have anyway. Jose hated children.

The boy straggling slowly at the tail end of the line irritated him too. The child stared up at him with those soulful black eyes like he could see right through Jose.

Bah. By nightfall, they would be almost there.

Jose snapped his whip again.

Its brass-tipped tail slashed against the buttocks of a squaw. She yelled an Indian curse at him but picked up her pace. This was certainly a lot more fun than herding cattle.

The line of prisoners was being driven hard and they were parched for water, but still the men kept urging them forward toward the mountains.

They were allowed to halt at the pass. By then it was twilight. The women were given several canteens of water to pass around. The pale-faced soldiers conferred with two more men who had been waiting at the pass with whips and horses.

Tortoise saw his aunt shiver violently.

They were going to be force-marched through the night.

Once they were on the other side of the pass, Tortoise was sure he would not have the opportunity to escape. He was not sure what a solitary, slow boy could do, but he had to try. He would make his father Brave Eagle proud, even if he had to die to do it.

"*Aiyee*," he whispered softly to his aunt and her

friend, the one with the baby. "I see the men's eyes. I see that they are not happy to have one so small as I. Perhaps I can be so slow they leave me."

"You will die out there all alone, Tortoise. You are not swift enough or smart enough to live by yourself. You stay with me."

"No," the boy said firmly. "I will get to Cochise. I will tell our Indian fathers who are still free what had happened. You must let me go."

His aunt shrugged. "I have no power over my own life. Do what you will. We are all finished."

So when the men spurred their horses and cracked their whips, Tortoise was the very last in line. He pretended he had twisted his ankle. It was a big risk.

The infant started to wail. His mother had taken the short break to nurse the thirsty child. Now his mother was being driven forward. The baby bawled lustily.

By now, Santos and Manuel had joined the captors. Five men to keep the slaves in line — and all were anxious to get their charges into a corral and celebrate.

"Make them move!" the long nose ordered.

Grumbling under his breath, Santos wheeled his horse to the boy and screamed at him in Spanish. He screamed at the infant.

The only effect this had was to make the child cry louder. Tortoise limped as if he was making an effort and fell to the earth.

Santos paused, considering.

He could shoot them, but what was the use? He called to the others, "The boy will not make it unless he rides on horseback."

"The hell with him," Tibbs yelled back. "He is not

worth so much anyway."

"Stop that baby from crying!" Crawford shouted, "or I will put a bullet through his heart. Damned commotion."

So Santos dismounted and grabbed the child from his mother. He tossed it to the startled Indian boy like tossing a sack of grain.

Let the weaklings cling to each other as they died out here. Santos was not as cruel as the others. He had babies at home. He uttered an oath and straddled his horse. Soon, the line was moving again.

Tortoise caught the bawling infant in his arms.

He had not been prepared for this development. He huddled and watched the others trudge on out of sight. He hugged the child to him as if it was a doll. After a time, the baby exhausted himself with crying and slept.

Tortoise was not about to travel through the dreaded dark. If the One Who Made All Things was watching out for him, he and the child would live.

Otherwise, they would die.

It was that simple. Tortoise was slow, but he understood simple things. What was meant to happen would happen. He would do his part. He knew how to gather cactus and slake his thirst. He knew that the chief who was called Cochise was somewhere out there, away from the soldiers.

Also, he had been crafty when it was his turn with the canteen. He had hidden it between his legs where the men would not find it. That was why he could walk no further. And the vessel was still one quarter full.

The child was a worry, but also a comfort.

Tortoise snuggled up to its small body and slept.

When he woke, he was not surprised to see an Indian dressed in the Apache breechclout of his people standing over him. Tortoise had been certain that the Indian was one who would lead him to Cochise.

What did surprise him was the beast the Indian led. It was taller than a man and had a hump on its back. It had mean teeth and sneering lips.

It must, Tortoise thought, possess some great magic.

Since the fierce looking brave spoke mostly in a tongue Tortoise had never heard, he used sign language to communicate.

The brave scowled in anger at Tortoise's story, but the scarred hands he laid on the boy and child were gentle and kind. By now, the child cried from thirst. The strange Indian showed Tortoise how to make a wet rag of broadcloth so the infant could suckle water.

The man and boy made signs for a long time.

Tortoise was very proud.

The Indian from a far land did not seem to think Tortoise was slow and stupid. He thought Tortoise was very brave and swifter than the eagle.

The problem, they agreed, was to get the child to one who could nurse it. They spoke man to man about the ways this could be done.

Cochise's band was very far, Tortoise learned.

But the reservation was not so very far, and the boy might find one who could help. Tortoise would never dare talk back to a brave of his own tribe, but this foreign redman was different.

Tortoise told him that the soldiers were bad. He agreed that he might get the child to a wetnurse, but that would not help his people.

The Indian whose name was Glidinghawk thought for a long time. He talked about one who was named Fox, a white man and a soldier. Fox was not bad.

It was almost too much for Tortoise, but he listened and what Glidinghawk said made sense. At least Tortoise could save a boy child of his people, and that was a brave and fine thing.

Tortoise was to take the child on the great humped beast and ride to where the sun set. There, he would come to the Fort Apache Reservation.

First, he would give the boy child to a squaw whose milk flowed. There were many there who would help. But if a soldier asked where Tortoise came from on the strange beast, he would draw his head back in his shell and say nothing.

He would carry with him a letter written by Glidinghawk.

He would ask for the white man named, like an Indian of cunning, Fox. If he could find Fox, he would give him this letter.

If he could not, he was to burn it in the nightly campfire and live a long life without bitterness. Tortoise was a brave and honorable Chiricahuan of many fine deeds. His children's children would hear tales of the day he rode the camel to save an Indian child.

So, with great misgivings, Tortoise let the Indian Glidinghawk pacify the babe with a wet rag and strap the child on his back.

He accepted help mounting the beast whose name was Mighty Hump. He learned how to tug the reins and keep his seat on the tall beast.

Tortoise lumbered away with both joy and sadness in

his heart. He was very small and very slow. This land was very big and fierce. The animal he rode was very big and fierce.

But he knew in his heart that this was as it should be. If the child could survive for the next five hours and Tortoise could keep his seat on the beast who was built like no other, he would become known as One Who Does Brave Deeds.

CHAPTER FOURTEEN

Glidinghawk watched the boy ride off toward the Fort Apache reservation. He hoped that Tortoise could manage. He was a brave boy, but so small, and the camel was a fiesty beast.

During their brief journey, Glidinghawk had begun to suspect that this was not the camel's first contact with man, but he would never know for sure. Besides, Glidinghawk recalled that the old shaman had told him never to question a gift from the gods.

He only hoped that Mighty Hump was the gift of salvation for the boy and the child as well.

Glidinghawk had done what he felt was right, sending that message to Fox. Again, there were so many ifs . . . but if Tortoise managed to deliver the letter, and if Fox was using his brains on this mission, Glidinghawk might expect help before fifty or more Apaches were sold into slavery.

The number was staggering.

Tortoise had outlined what had happened very clearly. Glidinghawk wept inside for his Indian brothers and sisters. His anger welled up in him and made his fingers itch to kill. Vengeance was too honorable a word for what he wanted.

The trail the captors and their slaves left was a clear path to follow. Glidinghawk's biggest decision was whether he could brace the outlaws—Mexicans *and* profiteering soldiers—by himself, or if he should attempt to get help.

But from where?

Although his hands were camel-bitten and swollen from the cactus barbs, they were quite capable of pulling a trigger. And his anger was so great he wanted to strangle the slavers in man-to-man combat and watch them suffer. His anger gave him strength—but it could also make him careless.

Without help, though, Glidinghawk's chances were slim. But he had come this far. From Tortoise's report, there were at least five men herding the new cargo of slaves. There would be more back at the hideaway.

There was nobody else for Glidinghawk to turn to.

Fort Apache was the only garrison within reasonable distance, and there, he knew, he would be wasting his time. Most of the soldiers, from what he surmised, were being bribed, paid off by either Crawford or Tibbs.

From the detailed description Tortoise had given, which included the chevrons on the Americans' uniforms, Glidinghawk was sure that that was who the two men were. The original report from Lt. Col. Amos Powell had most likely been accurate.

True, Glidinghawk should alert Fox, but he had taken care of that by sending the boy to the reservation.

Unfortunately, for the moment, it looked like he was on his own. *Proceed cautiously and scout out the enemy fortress*, Glidinghawk said silently to himself. *Then move in for the kill.*

This was, of course, insanity.

But one man had the power to irritate and annoy, like a single mosquito. It was the best he could do.

Under the cover of night, Glidinghawk approached the enemy camp from the west. He was on foot but armed. His backpack, still heavy with gold, had been hidden in some rocks, so he could maneuver freely. His Peacemaker was holstered by his side. He carried the Remington. His knife was in his high moccasin.

Glidinghawk had garbed himself in his buckskins. He had washed himself—a luxury after his time in the desert. In case he was spotted, he would look like an army scout, and that, he thought, might make Crawford and Tibbs very nervous.

When he reached the outer perimeter of the camp, he came upon a snoring guard. It was Santos. Glidinghawk had no way of knowing that this was the man who had let the boy and the baby live rather than shoot them.

Glidinghawk's razor-edged knife sliced through the man's throat before he could waken. Glidinghawk certainly did not want to change clothes with the Mexican, who in any event was far shorter and squatter than he was, but he did take his sombrero. Its distinctive shape silhouetted in the dark might come in handy.

There were rowdy sounds coming from the camp.

The central building was little more than a shack of earth and rocks, but it appeared impenetrable. The walls of natural material were thick. Windows caught the breeze, but they were too small to afford Glidinghawk a view of what was transpiring inside.

He could hear loutish voices and the thin wail of a woman, though. She was an Indian.

To the left, up a dusty path, was the corral. The prisoners huddled there. Two men with metal revolvers glinting on their hips guarded it. They appeared to be sleepy and lackadaisical.

Along the path was another shack, windowless, half dug into the hillside. Glidinghawk wondered if it could be the outhouse before realizing that the Mexican slavers were not that civilized.

Horses were tied to a hitching post in a lean-to. If Glidinghawk was not mistaken, he recognized the longer, leaner lines of two cavalry mounts among them.

Crawling over rocks and scrub, Glidinghawk's inclination was to take a closer look before formulating a plan. He was positive Celia and Landrum were prisoners somewhere in the compound. If he could get them out, all three of them would need horses.

Or pack mules.

Faith, Hope and Charity slept humbly beside the soldier's two geldings and the Mexican ponies. Glidinghawk had had no great attachment to the mules, but now it was like meeting old friends he thought were long dead or gone. It boded well, he thought.

"You hear anything?" Manuel asked Jaime, who was the other guard on the Apaches. Manuel was unhappy. He would much rather be celebrating with the others. He preferred to be teamed with Santos. They understood each other. Jaime was different and a loner.

"No," Jaime lied.

Jaime had been upset when the two Americans were

discovered and brought to camp. He had hoped they had some great plan to bring Sexto Diaz down. The woman was very lovely, Jaime thought, although she sometimes looked so far away and spoke like a child who lacked a grown woman's mind.

Jaime had been sad, but he had also been clever. When Sexto threatened to beat and rape the fair-skinned woman, Jaime had started a rumor. He had told everyone that the old man back in Sonora, the old man who bought Saguaro Flower, had a great fortune left.

"Yes, old Rodriguez, he told me that the Apache maiden was fine, but he would give his life savings in gold for a fair-haired virgin . . ."

The ruse had worked.

An Indian girl had been used in Celia's place, not once but many times, by all of the men . . . all except Jaime, and Santos who had been sent out to guard the hills.

Jaime had prayed to the Virgin, this time for deliverance for the strange couple who had been captured. His enemies were not the Americans. He hoped that others would come along and rescue them, killing Sexto in the process.

Then Jamie could take credit for saving the red-haired one's virginity. He and his sister Carmen would be free. Perhaps the Americans would offer Jaime a reward.

So Jaime lied and said he heard nothing and buried his head in daydreams of what might happen. He felt close to the strange white woman, who had smiled at him when he untied her wrists before locking her in the small shack.

What did worry him was the conference Tibbs and Crawford were having with Sexto right now. They were going to decide whether to shoot the man named Landrum or try to hold him for ransom.

At least that's what Jaime thought he had heard. At first, Sexto was going to stick a knife in the back of the tall, lean American — he said he would not waste a bullet. Sexto boasted of how swift he was with a knife.

Jaime knew Sexto liked to use a knife almost as much as a whip. The slaver was the son of a butcher, and he laughed from deep in his belly when he got an opportunity to slash a man. Jaime himself had scars to prove it — from both the wrong end of a rawhide whip and from the honed blade of the sadistic son of a she-dog.

But Landrum had claimed he had gold to trade for his life. Gold that only he had access to . . . a boast that made Jaime wonder about the cougar's cave he had seen the couple hiding in.

The men laughed at Landrum. Sexto had taken the pointed end of his blade and twisted it into the flesh of Landrum's neck, drawing a small point of blood. The tall man had gulped like a toad and turned his pockets inside out. True, there were gold coins tumbling to the earth floor.

So maybe there was more gold.

But Madre de Dios! Once Sexto got his hands on the gold, the man who called himself Landrum would die. The soldiers, the long nose and the other short, fat one, would see to it. They distrusted one of their own kind far more than they distrusted the Mexicans.

Jaime could not say why he was drawn to the Americans, except that the woman was beautiful and the man had eyes like few Jaime had seen. Dark and piercing, they seemed to have compassion and honesty in them. Jaime was not used to a look like that, but he dimly sensed that was what it was.

Jaime was so lost in his thoughts he did not notice that Manuel had drifted away. Well, Manuel was well liked by Sexto, and could get away with sneaking off for a drink. Jaime was not, and he always had to be on the alert—more for Sexto and his men than from outside threats.

The slave women were not much trouble. They were too weary after the march. They lay together on the ground, crooning to one another. The corral was built strongly, of beams that had been carted over the mountains. Like penned beeves, they were secure.

Still, after a time, Jaime began to wonder what had happened to Manuel. They were supposed to check with one another from time to time. He took his pistol and cocked it before wandering around the edge of the corral.

Sure enough, he saw Manuel up there, sleeping as usual. A sombrero hid his face. The man was a stupid brute. He could have picked a better spot for a siesta than the shoulder of rock between the corral and the stable.

Ah. If Sexto found Manuel sleeping, Jaime would be the one to get in trouble. He would awaken Manuel. He would kick the brute in his manhood . . . or at least he would like to. It would not be wise. He would only frighten Manuel a little.

Three feet from Manuel's body, he lowered the barrel of his pistol. He would place its single empty eye against Manuel's forehead and then shout, *"Arriba."*

As he did so, though, Manuel's bullet-shaped head slumped sideways. The hat fell off his head. Jaime felt strong hands grasping his neck from behind and digging in until the stars began to come out in front of his opened eyes. He saw the gleam of a blade.

With the last of his strength, Jaime rasped, "The white woman and Landrum . . . argh . . ."

Glidinghawk's knife halted in midair.

He turned Jaime so the lithe Mexican was pinned to the ground, his windpipe still being strangled. In Spanish—the language the man had spoken—Glidinghawk asked, "What of them? Where are they?"

Jaime's voice labored. He knew the Indian would kill him in an instant if he tried to call out. He was on this man's side—perhaps. If only he could let the Indian know it.

"In the shack . . . the woman . . . beautiful . . . Sexto will not kill her . . . the other . . . Landrum . . . they . . . I can help . . . argh . . . please."

Glidinghawk had a split second in which to consider. If logic ruled, he would slice the Mexican guard's throat and leave him here with the other dead bandelero. That would eliminate one more enemy.

But Glidinghawk had not been running on logic. That camel was not logic. Avoiding the false step on the mesa when he came up against the Apache sentry had not been logic. Knowing that he would find Celia and Landrum here was not logic. Some greater power was guiding him—if only he knew in what direction!

He loosened his neckhold. He stared into the Mexican's eyes. He felt the pain and fear buried within the man he had a life-and-death grip on. He felt he needed this man on his side.

"Why would you help me?" he asked in a voice as whispery and terrifying as a silken noose.

Jaime took a long breath. Glidinghawk watched the air relieve his oxygen-starved lungs. It could be a prelude to shouting for help, but the Indian merely waited.

"Sexto, the leader, he is my brother-in-law," Jaime said, his words strained from the roughness in his throat. "He is no good for my sister and no good for me. I hate the son-of-a-dog. Every day I pray to the Virgin that he will die. He lives and grows fatter. When the American two came, I thought they would get him, but they were caught."

"So you think I will kill him for you?" Glidinghawk asked, amused in spite of himself. "Why don't you do it yourself?"

Jaime was nothing if not transparent. "Because I am very yellow-bellied," he said honestly. "I am afraid of him and of his men. They are all killers. I have never killed a man."

"Are you willing to start?" Glidinghawk asked.

Jaime trembled violently. To kill was better than being killed, no? And if he refused, Jaime knew that the Indian's best choice would be to kill him before he could get in the way.

"*Si, señor*," Jaime rasped.

"Are there any more guards out here now, or are the men all inside getting drunk?" Glidinghawk asked.

"There is Santos in the hills," Jaime reported.

That, Glidinghawk thought, must be the one I murdered. "And in there?"

"Mexicans and soldiers both. They will be checking on us, on Manuel and me — and maybe they grow bored and want a fresh woman, no?"

"And the captive Americans?"

"In that building. But the lock and hasp it is very strong, and only Sexto has the key."

"He has it on him? Inside where they celebrate?" Glidinghawk prodded. "Exactly how many are there?"

"Two American soldiers, bad men, and Sexto and Jose. Jose, he has the meanness of many men."

"Can you get Sexto outside by himself—with the key?" Glidinghawk asked urgently.

Jaime took out his rosary beads and began to mumble to himself. He was so scared a strong, unmistakable odor was coming from him—and it was only part of his sheer, paralyzing terror.

CHAPTER FIFTEEN

It wasn't much of a plan, Glidinghawk knew. It was liable to be a bloody massacre. He was scared deep inside. If it didn't work, they were all dead—Celia, Landrum and himself. Glidinghawk knew he would have to handle the rough stuff himself, and he was not fighting for his life alone.

"Jaime, I want you to go back to your guard duty," Glidinghawk told the trembling Mexican. "Pretend nothing has happened. Later, I'll need you to call out a few words for me."

Jaime nodded without enthusiasm.

Glidinghawk arranged Manuel's dead body in a sleeping pose again, and covered his head with the sombrero. Unless anyone came very close, the blood drying blackish and sticky on the man's dead body did not show. He again looked as if he was sleeping.

Time . . . that's what Glidinghawk hoped for.

Time to alert Landrum and Celia that help was on its way, time for the bandeleros and their American cohorts to get drunker, time to get horses saddled and ready.

The odds were looking better.

Two to four at the moment, but the four slave-dealing men were heavily armed and would not hesitate to kill. And although the Omaha sensed that Jaime was on his side, the cowardly young man was not a warrior.

If only Glidinghawk had Landrum on his side, he knew he could blow this whole enemy encampment sky high. But freeing Landrum was a major problem. Glidinghawk darted in back of the prisoners' shack and tested its adobe walls. They were solid, too solid to break through without a major excavation.

He considered blowing the lock off the closed door to the shack, but that presented a risk he was not prepared for — yet. The men who were celebrating would be all over him before he could finish the job.

The Indian could see that the holding shack was the next thing to be buried alive. Because it was built into the mountain — its back wall was formed by dug-out rock and earth — it was probably not broiling hot during the day. But it was closed off from the fresh air.

After being locked in there, would Landrum be in any shape to run or to fight? Glidinghawk was certain Celia would not be. Most likely, she was still touched by that blow on her head, which the stress of capture could only have added to.

The door was a thick barrier of wood, probably hauled in over long, dry miles. Glidinghawk tested the lock with his fingers and found it fast, as formidable as the lock on a strongbox.

He knocked softly against the splintered, weather-beaten wood and called out, "Landrum . . . Celia?"

He thought he heard a shuffling from inside. It could have been a rat. He knocked again.

Glidinghawk heard a weak voice, a man's voice. At first, it did not seem like it belonged to Landrum. It was too beaten and lifeless. It was barely more than a moan — a questioning moan.

"It's me, Glidinghawk."

"No . . . it can't be."

"Dammit, it is so. Listen. I am armed. I am going to get you out of there. Be ready."

"You're real?" Landrum asked.

The Omaha knew what had happened. He had seen things like this before. How many days had Landrum and Celia been captives here? Four? Five? Locked in without light for most of that time, Landrum had lost his grip on reality.

"Yes, it is me. Please, try to get yourself together. When I open this door, I want you and Celia to run for the stables."

The thick door between them made communication difficult, but Glidinghawk thought he had gotten through. His main message needed few words: I am here. There is hope.

Next, Glidinghawk slipped into the stables like a wraith and saddled up four mounts. The beasts whinnied. Faith kicked him. On the way out, he saw Jaime cowering with fear by the corral and waved. The Mexican waved back uncertainly.

Certainly, Glidinghawk had considered freeing the Apache slaves and ordering them to run for the hills. But 40 females who spoke a language he was not proficient in were more than he could handle. He did creep up to them, and attempt to sign a message with his hands.

A young Indian woman who had been lying on her

back staring up at the stars startled when he called, "*Ayie* . . . psss . . . come here."

She turned her head hopelessly in his direction. Her long black hair was braided and hung way past her slender waist. Her black eyes were dulled, but they widened at seeing an Indian man.

He signed that there might be gunfire. He asked her to tell the others, should they wake, to stay calm. He was going to free them later . . . unless he was killed.

The nubile maiden signed back that she understood. Inside, she thought it was like a dream, and was not sure if the strange redman was real. Whoever he was, she knew he was not a Paiute, though. So if she heard shots fired, and saw fighting, she would tell the others. She riveted her gaze back on the far-off, mysterious stars.

Jaime came over and whispered in Spanish, "My heart, it is very fast. It tells me to run. I am very afraid."

Glidinghawk understood that the Mexican was telling him that he could not be relied on. But damnit, he needed Jaime. A flash of irritation shot through him as he repeated, "I need you to call Sexto outside."

Having the cooperation of the man was more than Glidinghawk had hoped for, if only it lasted for the next step of his plan.

This camp was run in a sloppy fashion—one of the pluses as far as Glidinghawk was concerned. Incredibly, he had killed two and gotten the cooperation of a third. From here on in, it would not be so easy.

He fell to his belly and crawled up to the main shack. It was one large room with bunks in one corner, a kitchen of sorts and a rough-hewn table to eat and drink at.

Slurred voices, laughter, the clink of glasses, and the weeping of the captive Chiricahuan maiden formed a medley of greed, drunkenness and lust.

Four men . . . four deadly rivals.

Glidinghawk knew the ground rules that had been laid out when he was hired as an undercover operative. He knew he was not officially empowered to kill. Just as certainly, he knew he would — except he wanted one of the soldiers alive so he could get the information on the others, back at Fort Apache, who had cooperated in this scheme.

But first, he must get Sexto. The bandeleros not only had the key that would free Landrum and Celia, but he was the key to this entire operation. Overhearing the shenanigans inside the slaver's place was not getting Glidinghawk any closer to his goal. He must begin to act.

Crawling back 20 feet from the entranceway — which was closed and bolted from the inside — Glidinghawk raised his Remington and fired into the air.

Then he waited, rifle recocked.

The men scrambled to their feet.

It was Sexto's camp, and there was no way either Crawford or Tibbs was going to get himself embroiled in the Mexicans' problems. Not when they had been paid off only moments before. The slaves were now Sexto's problem. He owned them.

Jose opened the door and yelled, *"Que? Que paso?"*

Glidinghawk raised his arms, motioning for Jaime to speak — but the man had disappeared from his post.

Jaime had run past the hills to the gorge where he suspected the gold was hidden. He had not waited around to help. He had told the Indian he was a coward. He had been honest in his own fashion. He was incapable of doing what Glidinghawk had asked of him.

Glidinghawk waited only a second. He would have to speak himself—that was his alternative, but far from foolproof. He had known Jaime was more woman than man.

The Indian's Spanish was flawless, and he knew the Mexican intonation. He had been listening carefully, both to Jaime and the dangerous men who drank to celebrate the capture and selling of others.

In Spanish he answered, "Much trouble. I think a soldier comes through the hills—and Manuel is asleep on the job."

Glidinghawk had elaborated enough. If Jose was drunk enough, he would not notice that Glidinghawk's voice was deeper and smoother than Jaime's thinner, reedy one.

"So you take care of it."

"I have never shot a man."

"Dumb son of a she-dog. Wake Manuel, don't shoot him."

"But the soldier who spies?"

"Argh. I will report this. Let his own kind take care of him, eh? For myself, it is time to drink and make love."

Damn. This was not going according to plan. Sexto was not showing his greasy face. The men were almost impossible to get to if they kept to the enclosed hideaway. And if he shot Jose now, the others would make a fortress of the building. It would be three swift guns against a solitary man.

The hell with this action, Glidinghawk decided as the man named Jose stumbled back inside He strode angrily over to the prisoners' shack and blasted a rifleshot right through the lock. It sank on its hinges but held. Glidinghawk squeezed off another shot.

He was in a bad position. He was a sure-shot target if any of the men inside was clear-headed enough to figure out what was happening. He had only seconds.

With his battered hands, he tugged at the searing hot metal of the lock. It came apart in his hands. From inside, Landrum heaved mightily at the door. It opened a slit.

Landrum darted out — then kicked the door shut behind him. Celia was still inside. She would be safer there.

Glidinghawk took his white brother's hand and they ran back behind the stables. He supplied Landrum with the loaded Peacemaker. Landrum was an excellent marksman with the handgun — though it was far from accurate at a distance.

Still, it made a great boom discharging into the enemy's fortress. Rifle barrels extended from the windows of the shack. Indian women shrieked from the human corral.

Realizing they were no longer under guard, the first captive to climb the corral fence started a mass exodus. The others clambered behind her, running for the safety of the hills.

This was the worst thing that could have happened, Glidinghawk realized. Standing ands running made every one of them a perfect target. And if they were not gunned down by a slaver's bullet in the back they would get caught in the crossfire.

Landrum realized the same thing. The older man looked like hell. His face was pinched, pale and haggard. The scar across his cheek stood out like a small albino snake. His narrowed eyes had trouble focusing.

He rallied, though. Landrum dashed around to the back hills, behind the shack, and started firing. It was a clever move. It diverted the slavers' attention from the fleeing maidens. His fury and the rapid chattering of the Peacemaker made it seem that many more enemies than two were closing in on the gang.

The situation was still desperate, though.

The superior gunpower of the men inside and their protected position meant they could outlast the two mosquitoes. Glidinghawk knew he would have to come up with a decisive move. Their ammunition was low.

It was a pleasure to be with Landrum again, especially in this tense situation. Landrum sensed what the Omaha was going to do. Glidinghawk exchanged the rifle for the Peacemaker.

Landrum fired repeatedly, keeping the men inside busy, their heads bobbing in and out of sight, rifles chattering, while Glidinghawk lit out in the opposite direction.

He scrambled to the windows on the other side, then threw himself down as the bullet sang above his head. It was a close call. He glued himself to a wall.

He saw the stock of a rifle edge out just inches from where he was flattened in wait. That was all he needed. He thrust his gun arm at the man who held the rifle and squeezed the trigger. Brains splattered.

Fired by this partial victory, Glidinghawk lost all caution. He shot again into the house and wounded

Sexto in the back. A fat, short man wearing soldier blue pulled an Apache woman in front of him for cover and ducked under a bunk.

Captain Crawford was as much of a coward, but he was not swift enough. He was blasted through the shoulder by Landrum, who was storming the place, and in the kneecap by Glidinghawk, who was piling in through the other window. Honorius fell writhing in agony.

The man under the bed yelled, "Don't shoot. I will give you gold — anything. Don't kill me."

Glidinghawk dragged the man out by his thinning hair. He signed to the girl that everything would be all right, but he could see from the crazed look in her opaque black eyes that nothing would be all right for her, ever again.

Glidinghawk kicked Tibbs in the groin. Crawford was already in so much pain he could not feel any more. The others — Sexto and Jose — were dead.

Which, if Jaime had been telling the truth, left him as the last of the gang. Glidinghawk thought they should find him — later.

For now, he went to get Celia while Landrum collapsed on one of the bunks. The imprisonment had eaten away at the older man's strength. He gave Glidinghawk a brief grin of victory, but it was clearly an effort.

Celia murmured, "Thank God," when Glidinghawk came through the door. She breathed deeply. The stuffiness and darkness had gotten to her.

Leaning on Glidinghawk, she allowed herself to be led to the bandeleros' hideaway. She immediately rushed to Landrum and sank into his arms.

The captives had all disappeared—all but the girl who had been raped and abused until she was almost catatonic. In the dawn's light, Glidinghawk and Landrum would have to try to find the Apache women, to help them get back to the reservation.

Tonight, they needed rest.

Although the chore was distasteful—though not as bad as dragging the bloodied corpses outside, which Glidinghawk did—Landrum got out his pocketknife and dug the bullets out of Crawford's flesh. He bandaged the captain's wounds, both shoulder and kneecap, so roughly that the greedy soldier passed out.

The army would have a chance to court-martial Crawford after all. The other piece of scum, Tibbs, too. Powell's Army would have locked their enemies in the airless shack, with the corpses, but it was too much trouble.

"How did you make it out of the desert?" Landrum finally asked, once the soldiers were chained to bunks—not that Crawford was up to attempting escape, but the other one might. Besides, there was something satisfying about tying the rope around Honorius' wrists—tightly.

Glidinghawk appeared to think for a long time before answering. When he finally did, neither of his partners believed him. "On the back of a camel," he said.

"Glidinghawk, I am too tired for games," Celia said. "Tell us how you survived."

The Omaha proceeded to tell them about the cactus and the grubs, and riding his fever out in the wilderness. He filled them in on catching the camel—they were beginning to believe him—and told them about the Indian boy with the baby.

Celia was asking him for more details when all three of them heard the beat of horsehooves bearing down in their direction. At least one horse was galloping right into the camp. Two warning shots were fired by its rider.

A prissy, familiar voice rang out.

"Come out with your hands up. You are dealing with the US Army—and you are all under arrest."

CHAPTER SIXTEEN

"Is this the cavalry rushing to the rescue?" Celia asked drily.

Landrum laughed—far louder than the situation warranted. It was good to hear Celia come back to life, even if it was in the early morning hours and, aside from other afflictions, all three of them were half dead from exhaustion.

"Fox!" Glidinghawk sighed unhappily. "The Apache boy must have gotten through safely and passed the message to him. I guess we'd better call him in here."

"The idiot!" Landrum said. "He's a sitting duck out there in the moonlight. He must have had his head tucked up his . . . excuse me, Celia, you know what I mean . . . when God passed around brains."

Outside, the cavalry mount snickered and pawed the ground. His sleek coat was dappled with silver light. Glidinghawk heard other horses in the background. Strange, that some sounded shoed, while there was also a muffled beat of unshod ponies.

Fox called out one more time, "Come out with your

hands up. I'm going to count to ten—and start shooting."

Landrum went to the window.

It was Fox all right. Landrum could see him almost as clearly as if it were day. Fresh-faced, uniform buttoned to his stiff neck, face red from exertion and heat. He held his seat and pointed a rifle barrel in the direction of the hideaway.

"Are you going to rush out and kiss him hello?" Glidinghawk asked Landrum.

"Hell no, he's liable to shoot me."

"I'll call out to him. Surely he'll know it's us," Celia said. "If you hadn't killed or disarmed Sexto and the other men, Fox would be dead by now."

"Wait," Glidinghawk cautioned. "I think that is the idea. I'm sure there are other soldiers with him, hiding in the hills, and I don't think they're on our side. They probably expect Sexto to shoot Fox."

"Why us?" Landrum said to nobody in particular.

Celia blew out the candles, all but one that flickered dimly in a corner of the room by the bunks. Now, it appeared even lighter outside.

Like the others, she was remembering how Second Lt. Preston Kirkwood Fox had almost gotten them all killed on their first mission at Fort Griffin.

"History repeats itself," Glidinghawk mumbled softly. He stole to the window, next to Landrum, and peered out.

"One!" Fox shouted, his voice quavering loudly.

"Should I call him?" Celia asked, standing in back of Landrum so close he could feel her warm breath brush his shoulder.

Glidinghawk noticed, too, but he understood. Surviving together had bonded Celia and Landrum in a manner that went deeper than love or sex. Later, Glidinghawk would think about it, about the changes they had all gone through. Now there was too much else to handle.

"Two!" Fox said. The metallic gleam of his weapon pointed straight at the hideaway window.

"Shh, Ceil," Glidinghawk said. "We have to assume there are other soldiers out there, and they are in Crawford's pay. I want you to scream, so he knows it's you. Then I'll speak."

Landrum's heavy eyebrows raised. "It's worth a try. You got your Spanish act polished?"

"*Si, señor*," Glidinghawk said. Landrum did not smile. This was grim. Both men knew that they were far outnumbered, assuming this fiasco was anything like the rest of this twisted mission.

Up against armed, fresh soldiers, they were finished. Fox was a decoy, a sitting duck like the ones Landrum had hunted as a boy, squarely in the middle. This was too tricky for his liking.

"Scream now," Landrum whispered.

"Three . . ." Fox continued his count as Celia let out with a shriek. "Help! Please help me. The Mexicans have me prisoner!"

Her fright sounded real enough.

Tibbs, who had been bound but not gagged, started to shout. Landrum whirled around and slammed into the side of his head with the butt of the Remington. The man rolled over on his bunk, out.

Glidinghawk called out in Spanish, trying to imitate the late slaver's guttural voice, "We have the white woman as a captive. You shoot and we will kill her."

"Four . . . five . . ."

"The idiot doesn't understand Spanish!" Landrum said.

"Celia Louise Burnett," Glidinghawk shouted, giving her name the Spanish intonation.

"Six . . . seven . . . eight," Fox counted, his finger squeezing slightly on the trigger.

Landrum and Glidinghawk moved away from the window. They gave each other a brief look, as if to say, *What now?*

The thoughts running through the Omaha's head were these: *If I am forced to kill Fox to save Celia and Landrum, I will be strong and do it. The army might put me up in front of the firing squad for it, but those are army men out there. They plan to kill Fox, but not by their own hand. They are the dregs, the evil ones, the money-grubbing ones. They value no life but their own.*

The soldiers, well out of gunshot range, could not understand why the bandeleros did not put a bullet through Fox's heart. The stupid army inspector was in clear view.

Crawford and Tibbs must be inside, the men thought. Surely one of them would pull the trigger. None of them had met Sexto Diaz. Their part in the slaver scheme was to round up the human flesh and turn it over to Crawford and Tibbs. But surely the Mexican would be grateful to them — added dollars or pesos grateful. When Fox had approached them, they were clever. Major Hardy had played his hand well, taking along men who were in Crawford's pay.

The men left back at Fort Apache who were not involved knew nothing, other than there was some trouble Fox suspected in the hills.

It would be neat. Once Foxe was killed—and Sexto had shown his gratitude—they would return to the fort. Hardy knew what he would say, had it all planned in his mind.

That Injun boy? Well, he was right about Indian trouble and one of them Apaches had a rifle, killed the army inspector dead. But we managed, killed a few. Guess we'd better be tougher when we round up the rest of them savages.

But why didn't Sexto or Crawford or somebody shoot the dumb fellow? What were they waiting for?

"Te—"

"If you shoot they will kill me!" Celia shouted.

Using an atrocious Spanish accent, Glidinghawk said, "We weel keel thees woman unless you come to us weeth your hands een the air."

Silence. Tension.

A wracking breath from Fox, a slight tilt of his head, as if waiting for orders. From behind him, no sound, no support. The empty single eye of his rifle faltered toward the ground.

An exclamation, an oath that carried on the wind. There were others out there all right, and they couldn't figure this out. It was all right with them, though, if Fox walked right into the trap. Dead one way was as good as another.

Fox moved woodenly. He slid from the tall gelding. He refastened his rifle to the saddle and patted the horse on the rump. Unarmed, he walked to the sure death that awaited him in the slaver's hideaway.

Well, he would see Celia one last time. Once, she had saved his life. Fox had expected his fellow officers would do something to save him, but he was caught.

His life for Celia's . . . he owed her.

He saw the entrance to the adobe building open a crack. He wondered what his death would feel like. A quick bullet through the heart? A knife slicing across his jugular?

He squared his shoulders. Proper military bearing was important to him. It had been drummed into him often enough at West Point. His eyes focused straight ahead. He stepped inside.

"You silly fool," Celia hissed, and pulled him through the door.

His eyes widened. He could not comprehend what he was seeing—or whom. Glidinghawk patted him on the shoulder. Landrum snorted, quietly. "You are a wonder all right. How many killers did you sic on us this time?"

Dazed, Fox stared. His eyes bugged out. Sweat made a mustache on his upper lip, where wisps of hair were attempting to root.

He gazed from the two soldiers bound on the cots to the members of his undercover team. No bandit flew out of the shadows at him. "I brought help," he finally squeaked.

Landrum's hand balled into a fist and he swung. Glidinghawk caught Landrum's avenging arm. "No—not now! We can't afford to fight. Let me explain it to Lieutenant Fox."

The Indian's level voice calmed Landrum's blind fury. Glidinghawk was right: what was the point? They were in deep cowchips now, and knocking the sorry pantywaist out would only make it worse. They might be able to use Fox—maybe as armor. He had to do good for something.

"I take it you got my message," Glidinghawk said.

"Yes," Fox answered uncertainly. "I got here as soon as I could. And I brought help. I told Major Hardy at the fort and he picked some men for me. Will you tell me what's going on?"

Landrum paced the darkened room impatiently, slamming his fist into his palm. It made a whush-slam sound. His anger was barely under control.

"First," Glidinghawk said, talking as if Fox was a dimwitted child, "you knew that Crawford and Tibbs were involved in the slave ring."

Fox nodded. His cheeks were beginning to burn.

"Well, we can assume that Crawford was paying off other soldiers at Fort Apache, right?"

Fox nodded again. He started to whine, "But I couldn't come alone up against a whole gang."

Landrum exploded, "What's left of the whole gang is tied up in here—except the ones you brought along. You damned fool! Couldn't you see how they were setting you up to get yourself killed?"

"I, uh, I thought they were pushing me a little . . . I'm sorry."

"A helluva lot of . . ."

"Enough. The question is, what do we do now? How long before the soldiers out there come out of hiding? How do we make them believe that Sexto is still alive? How do we round them up?

"How many are there?" Landrum asked.

"Seven, besides me," Fox answered. "They are all armed with army-issue pistols, rifles and plenty of ammunition. Each one of them has a good horse. I don't even know all their names, only Major Hardy's and his aide's."

"Terrific," Landrum said sarcastically. "You brought quite a party."

"We are too quiet in here," Glidinghawk said. "Celia, scream when I fire this Peacemaker. Landrum, see if you can rouse Crawford. We need him to extend an invitation to his boys. Fox, get yourself armed. We need you, too."

"Thank you," Fox said humbly.

"Celia, I want you to get under one of the bunks, and stay there."

"Wait a minute," she protested. "I'm a good shot, too. And I'm not going to run off and let you protect me. It seems I've been doing too much of that lately."

"Yes, ma'am," Glidinghawk said.

Now that they all understood what they must do—including Fox—they moved with stealth and deadly grace. All of a sudden, it seemed like there were too damned many windows in the place. If the soldiers outside were suspicious, it might get difficult to cover them all.

Might? Hell, it would be impossible.

Their hope lay in getting the soldiers to walk right into the trap. From the looks of it, though, Crawford was past the point of cooperating—even with the knife blade Landrum had shoved up against a very vulnerable spot. The wounded captain drooled in fear and stammered before passing out again.

Tibbs was already out. He moaned when Glidinghawk shook him. So much for either of them. Glidinghawk would have to try his Sexto Diaz impersonation again.

Once they were braced and armed, Glidinghawk squeezed off a shot into a thin mattress. Its echo reverberated through the hills. Celia screamed her head off. Glidinghawk gave a triumphant victory shout. "Aha! We got the dog turd!"

They waited.

"You think they are on to us?" Landrum whispered when nothing happened.

"I'm not sure," Glidinghawk said. "Listen. Do you hear anything else?"

The thud-thud-thud, softly muffled, of many ponies carried through the waning night. "Did you run across any Indians on your ride here?" Landrum asked Fox.

Fox shook his head.

Celia said, "I didn't think Apaches rode at night."

Glidinghawk's carved idol face tightened, until the smooth, high planes of his cheek bones and his Mongolian-slanted eyes made him look like an ancient prophet.

"If they get angry enough, they will. The soldiers have pulled enough on them at night to change their ways. And it seems to me that fifty captives could add up to a heap of angry."

"Chiricahua?" Fox asked.

"Who else?" Glidinghawk said. "They are the ones whom the soldiers have been raiding. Cochise is one of the few strong warriors left. And they took his granddaughter Saguaro Flower. He isn't too happy, and he thinks we are the slavers."

"Are you sure you don't want to hide under the bunk?" Landrum asked Celia.

"What about the soldiers?" Fox asked.

"Your problem. You brought them," Landrum declared coldly.

Just then, they heard a commotion from outside.

A soldier let out a blood-curdling shriek—much more frightening than the one Celia had faked. Horses' feet, both shod and unshod, danced against the earth.

Major Hardy shouted, "Sexto! Crawford! Apaches out here. I'm coming in with my men. We'll have to fight them off."

Glidinghawk shouted gruffly in Spanish, "Hurry. My men await you."

His men looked at one another—one idiot soldier boy, one tired Texan, and one green-eyed girl whose freckles stood out like beacons.

The only other conscious person in the room, the girl who had been so cruelly used by Sexto and his men, came up silently behind Glidinghawk and tapped him on the shoulder.

In her own language, she whispered, "Give me a knife. I want to help you kill the blue coats."

She made signs with her hands. She spat on the floor to show Glidinghawk what she thought of the army men who had raided her band. Glidinghawk did not know it, but she was the aunt of the boy called Tortoise. Her name was Willow.

Glidinghawk reached down to his moccasin and handed her his knife. It had killed many times, and he was sure the woman was angry enough to use it to kill again.

Landrum told Glidinghawk, "I hope you know what you are doing. She might stab us in the back."

Glidinghawk answered tersely, "I feel inside that she will help us and we need all the help we can get. Besides, it's too late now."

The first of the armed soldiers hammered at the door, dodging Indian bullets and arrows. Another desperate man followed on his heels. Soon, there were five.

"Let us in, dammit!" Major Hardy shouted.

"Are we all ready?" Glidinghawk asked.

CHAPTER SEVENTEEN

The last soldier through the door fell flat on his face. From behind, an arrow had pierced his heart and lungs. Its tip was deeply buried in the enlisted man's flesh. Its shaft still vibrated. The soldier was dead. Glidinghawk kicked his body out the door before closing it.

Hardy was the first to reach safety — only as soon as he felt the Peacemaker digging into his ribs, he knew he wasn't safe.

"Soldiers, drop your weapons to the floor."

Landrum spoke. The others tensely covered the men. Only four soldiers were left of the original seven — four, and the ringleaders Crawford and Tibbs, who were out of commission.

Major Hardy's shock stunned him. For a moment, he could not speak. His sly eyes zoomed sideways, looking for a clever move. A white woman had a gun pointed directly at his head. A squaw brandishing a knife had his aide up against a wall. Her black, tilted eyes glared with hatred.

The other two soldiers were held at gunpoint by a tall, rough-looking man in buckskins and a savage Indian. Hardy's pistol clattered to the floor. Fox was standing in the midst of them, a rifle in his hand. Whoever they were, Fox was one of them, on their side.

"You can't do this," Hardy said. "Them Injuns will kill us all. We can make a deal."

"Like the deal you made to help me?" Fox asked bitterly. This, Fox knew, was his second defeat with Powell's Army. His guilt and shame were bottomless.

"Whatever else you are, you are a soldier," Hardy said. The major was grasping, trying for leverage. "You can't let them Apaches massacre us. You have it all wrong. It was them slavers we're after, not these people."

"It won't work, Hardy," Landrum said harshly. "You were setting up Fox's death. You're in on it and we know it."

Bullets zinged through the air outside. The Apaches had some guns—and even if they were single action weapons that needed to be reloaded after every shot, there were enough of them to make up for their lack of sophistication.

The door splintered as an arrow split dry wood. Bows and arrows were formidable weapons in skilled hands. Between rifles and archery, the Chiricahuans had the advantage.

The relentless sun was rising in the sky. The Chiricahuan warriors were growing bolder. It sounded like there were many scores of warriors out there.

"There's no point in arguing," Glidinghawk said. "All of you—Hardy, that means you and your men—get over by the bunks. Celia, you cover them. If any one of them so much as wipes his nose, shoot to kill."

Grumbling and pale with fear, the soldiers were herded over by Crawford and Tibbs. The Apache maiden Willow stood by Celia's side, watching the men she hated and feared out of eyes more menacing than a moonless night.

That left Glidinghawk, Landrum and Fox to fight the Chiricahua, if it came to that. Fox exchanged his pistol for a rifle and headed for the window.

"Stop!" Glidinghawk ordered.

Fox turned his head ever so slightly. By now, his actions were automatic, even in his daze. The enemy was outside. He was trained to fight. It was simple and uncomplicated—unlike the situation inside, where soldiers, one of them a fellow officer, had actually turned against him and set him up. His puzzlement did not last long.

"Goddammit!" Landrum exploded. "Listen to Glidinghawk."

"We have caused the Chiricahua enough death and misery," Glidinghawk said. "Besides, there are too many to fight. We will negotiate."

Fox had been around frontier posts long enough to know Indians do not negotiate. His current humility was only exceeded by his lifelong pomposity. In that grating, prissy voice of his, he began to recite, "Heathen cannot be reasoned with—"

"Who's going to reason?" Landrum said. His control was gone. "We will give them the soldiers—they won't have to reason to figure that one out."

Fox's jaw dropped open.

This was not done. Courts-martial, military arrests,

yes. But to actually turn US Army soldiers over to the Indians was blasphemy.

Glidinghawk nodded. "It is the only way, the only peace offering they will understand."

Hardy sobbed, "You can't. We're white men, all of us. We have to stick together."

"Speak for yourself, paleface," Glidinghawk said. His lips curled into a sneer. "I'm not white—and I'm willing to turn you over to them."

Action followed swiftly when an arrow sailed through the back window and lodged in an adobe wall. It missed the back of Celia's head by inches.

Willow saw and understood what was happening—almost. The veil of hatred that clouded her vision could only be lifted by revenge.

She knew she must help the strong brave who had rescued her and her people. She understood that the white man and the woman and the whey-faced young soldier were trying to help the Chiricahua. But the others? The hated blue coats?

Before anyone could stop her, she lunged for Crawford, who lay moaning on the bunk. With a swift flash of the blade, she plunged Glidinghawk's knife into the soldier's heart muscle. Blood spurted from an arterial vein and geysered into the air.

Tibbs was just coming to, just rising to consciousness. His eyelids fluttered. He woke with a start. He was trussed hand and foot. He recognized the men from Fort Apache. In a flash he also recognized that they were held prisoner.

As Willow grasped the handle of the knife and tugged it out of Crawford's convulsing form, Tibbs strained against his bonds. His face was wet with the perspiration of abject terror. He had used the squaw, had plunged his manhood into her . . . and now she was raising the blade high above her head with both hands to plunge into him.

Tibb's scream was high-pitched, frantic, and brief. The razor-sharp weapon sliced his abdomen open, cutting through the fabric of his uniform as if it were made of parchment. The pain was agonizing. Mercifully, he passed out once more . . . for the final time.

"We have to move!" Landrum was the first to tear his gaze away from the murdered men.

Hardy was extremely pale. He was murmuring fragments of long-forgotten prayers. A young enlisted man, not more than eighteen years old, fell on his knees and bowed his head.

Willow signed to Glidinghawk, "Now I can help you talk to my people. I will tell them that you are the brave who freed my sisters. I am ready."

She shouted out the window in the Chiricahuan dialect. All the Apache languages were of the Athapascan linguistic family, but the nuances and inflections of each tribe were different.

Glidinghawk understood only a little. It was very different from the Sioux, Omaha or Nez Perce languages he knew. But he understood the sudden silence that greeted her words and the absence of rifle shots and arrows.

Willow told him, as best she could, "They do not trust you, any of you."

Landrum picked up on this. "We will exchange the soldiers for our lives, tell them that."

Graceful, death-dealing hands fluttering like the

wings of a trapped bird, Willow tried to express that the exchange might not be enough. Her people must understand that Glidinghawk and the white man and woman came as friends and saviors.

"See if any of your people speaks Spanish," Glidinghawk said. Because of the proximity to the Mexican border, and the trading through the years, many Chiricahuan men had learned Spanish, but not English. If a trader was among the bands today, Glidinghawk could communicate—and he needed to desperately.

Sign language was universal with the Indians, but it was slow and unwieldly, especially for conveying complicated thoughts. To explain how Glidinghawk and Celia and Landrum came to be in the slavers' hideaway holding soldiers at gunpoint was complicated.

The soldiers huddled in terror. Celia's pistol was cocked and ready. The heavyset middle-aged soldier called Williams feinted to the right. Celia squeezed the trigger and shot him through the right arm. He was lucky—so far.

The Indian girl called out to her people. Finally, a voice answered, speaking rusty but serviceable Spanish. Glidinghawk's spirits rose.

In the language of the Conquistadors, he said, "Brothers, I am an Indian of a different tribe. It has been my job to free your people who were taken prisoner. My friends and I came to help, not to kill."

Shouting from this distance was not working well, but the man passed on Glidinghawk's message and called back, "Come to us and we will talk. Give us the soldiers. Bring the girl Willow who spoke to us."

Landrum told Glidinghawk, "I don't like this. They

might scalp you once they have the soldiers. Then what will Celia, Fox and I do?"

Glidinghawk answered, "We will all be killed otherwise, so we have nothing to lose. I will go."

"Wait," Landrum said. "Tell them you and Willow will go have a pow wow. Don't give them everything at once. Tell them if your talk works out, we will hand over the soldiers to them — or what's left of them."

Fox wiped his forehead. His head was swimming with fear. He saw the way the Apache squaw looked at him. He was one of them, the army men, at least to all appearances. When the fighting and killing started again, distinctions wore thin — and Fox was wearing a uniform.

As Glidinghawk called out his deal, Celia noticed Fox's trembling hands and terrified face. "Take off your uniform," she said, surprisingly gentle with him. "Go ahead, get that jacket and shirt off."

Landrum snorted. It was enough of a comment without words. Fox stripped to the waist and looked around, ashamed and uncertain. There was nothing for him to put on.

"Go ahead, over by the bunk. Sexto stored some possessions over there. Find something," Celia urged. "Anyone wearing a uniform is the enemy to the Apache."

"You are a disgrace!" Hardy hissed.

Celia's pistol waving in his face quieted him. Hardy's comment had the desired effect though, and made Fox feel bare and traitorous and cowardly. He hesitated, even after finding a dirty cotton shirt and raggedy trousers.

"I can't do this," he said. "Better to die like an army

181

man—"

"Shut up and change," Landrum snarled. Then, facing Glidinghawk, "Are they buying?"

"For a talk, yes. I'm not sure how the negotiations will go. Speaking of buying, do you still have your gold?"

"Hell, yes," Landrum said, "but it isn't here. Celia and I left it by the gorge, in a cave. You got your share?"

"I left mine with my backpack," Glidinghawk said.

"Sexto's gold?" Landrum queried.

"If I have to, I'll promise them everything, including money. We'll figure out how to get it later. In the meantime, find where Sexto and Crawford hid their cash and gold . . . and wish me luck."

Taking Willow's hand, Glidinghawk walked out the door with her. The sun was high in the sky. The drone of a hot summer day was in the air. A band of Indians waited for Glidinghawk by the stables. The war paint on their faces made them look like avenging spirits.

Landrum watched from the window.

He saw how straight and proud Glidinghawk stood. The Omaha appeared to be without fear or doubt. His entire stance was noble, head high, black hair which had grown long on this mission hanging straight to his shoulders, held back on his forehead by the Apache headband.

Although he was surrounded by painted warriors, it was Glidinghawk who commanded with his bravery and strength, his conviction that differences could be settled. The Chiricahuas seemed to respond to his presence.

The Spanish-speaking spokesman for the tribe said,

"Come. We have made a camp for one of our chiefs, back where the stream flows and the hills rise up out of the earth. He is waiting for you."

Single file, the Indians turned and walked on a faint path. Glidinghawk had a tall warrior in front of him, and another exceptionally large Chiricahuan in back of him. Their pace was fast but stately.

Willow walked beside a young man who shook his fist at her, and then hit her across the mouth with a loud whack. She whimpered, held her hand to her face, and fell in step behind him.

Glidinghawk saw that other braves ringed the hideaway. They were not going anywhere. Several bands had joined together for this attack on the slave camp. They wanted the blood of their enemies, and would make sure none escaped from the slavers' headquarters.

"Are the women who fled to the hills last night safe?" Glidinghawk asked the interpreter.

"We will talk later," the man said.

Glidinghawk noted that the Spanish-speaking Apache did not have the marks of respect and nobility on his bronzed cheeks. Probably, because the Indian Who Trades With Enemies had not lived in the traditional Indian ways, he was not much respected by the Chiricahua.

The rest of the journey was short and silent.

From the description Landrum and Celia had given him, Glidinghawk was sure this gorge was where they had taken refuge before Sexto's gang had captured them.

The two cottonwoods made a welcome path of green in the dusty landscape. In the distance, the sawtooth peaks of mountains shot up into the sky. Clouds hung there like strange, woolly mammoths.

Several wickiups had been hastily erected — not the willowbranched wickiups of a semi-permanent camp, but the hide covered frames of temporary shelters. Glidinghawk saw women milling by the small stream.

He thought he recognized the girl he had spoken with last night. He hoped it was she, for that would give him an added chance of convincing these skeptical Chiricahuas that he was a friend.

A friend? A knot of fear tightened in Glidinghawk's gut.

In the last several weeks, he did not know how many Apache braves he had killed. He remembered the mesa above a campsite almost as pleasant as this and the band attacking. He recalled the brave tumbling off the headland, and the others who were shot.

How many more had Glidinghawk and Landrum killed when they rescued Celia? And now, he was going to convince these people that he wished the Chiricahua long life and peace?

For a moment, Glidinghawk's attention was diverted. He saw up above the stream the tattered remnants of a man. The clothing looked familiar. It was Jaime.

Some braves were laying rocks ceremoniously over Jaime's body, although he was an enemy. They were anchoring his spirit to earth, so it would not roam in the night and come back to haunt them.

Looking more closely, Glidinghawk saw the streaked claw marks across Jaime's prone body. The Indians had not killed the cowardly Mexican. The slashes across his handsome face were from a giant cat, a cougar. The cougar had killed him.

The hungry snake of fear grew large in Glidinghawk's belly. He understood a cougar defending his territory. How much more right the Chiricahua had to defend theirs.

Glidinghawk wondered what he would do if he were one of these maligned bands of Apaches? Perhaps he, too, would kill, both the enemy who talked of peace but killed instead, and the other enemies waiting back at the hideaway.

"This way," One Who Trades With Enemies ordered.

Glidinghawk knew he was coming face to face with a chief. The man wore a band of eagle feathers in his hair. His manner was kingly.

"I am Naiche, son of Cochise," he said. "Father of Saguaro Flower."

"I have heard great things of the brave Cochise, your father," Glidinghawk acknowledged. "What I have been told of your daughter who has been sold into slavery saddens me, which is why I came to free the other women of your tribe."

One Who Trades With Enemies translated, his face neutral.

Naiche walked a step closer to Glidinghawk. He peered into Glidinghawk's eyes as if seeking the truth there. His own eyes smoldered in their sockets like angry fires.

Ringed around them, many braves watched and listened. Glidinghawk could feel their thoughts: The bright summer of the Indian was over, and they would wither away and die like the seasons while the white man grew like a spring blight on the land.

They could not stop this blight, for it would grow up

again and again all around them. But this little patch of evil nestled in the Gilas, with slavers and white people and a strange Indian brave, they could stomp out and destroy.

Their eagerness was almost a palpable force.

It grew like a rising wind when Naiche said, "I know you, Omaha. You stole into my camp and killed my brothers. And now, you talk of peace and deliverance."

CHAPTER EIGHTEEN

The leather headband Glidinghawk wore burned like a scarlet letter on his forehead. He had taken it from the sentry he had murdered outside of Naiche's camp. He wondered if the son of Cochise recognized it.

"Your braves raided my camp and stole the white woman," Glidinghawk said. "I had to make bad medicine to get her back. I did not want to kill, but you left me no choice."

Naiche was silent. Then he asked, "Who do you work for, that you travel with white men and a white woman? Are you only a pawn sent to destroy us, like the scouts used by the soldiers who have sold their Indian souls to the white men?"

"I work for one who wants peace," Glidinghawk explained. "His color is white, but he understands the sorrow of the red man. He told the Great White Father that many bad things happen to your people because of the bad soldiers."

Naiche spat on the ground in contempt.

"I do not blame you for trusting no one," Glidinghawk said. "I have freed your women. I have killed the men who would have them as slaves. I will give you the soldiers who sold your people."

Naiche asked Willow to speak. True, she was only a woman, but she had been there. She told Naiche that the Omaha spoke truth.

The Indian Chief stroked his beardless chin and thought. He wished his father was here, but Cochise was growing old and infirm. Cochise wanted to see his favorite granddaughter before he died.

Why, Naiche did not know. His daughter Saguaro Flower was but a slip of a woman, but dying men have strange wishes. Being a good son, Naiche should honor the request, if he could.

Naiche cared about his daughter, but he had manly things to think about. With Cochise's passing, the reins of power would fall to him. He did not know if he could bind the different bands of the Apache together in a common cause as his father had done.

Nor, Naiche realized, was uniting them to fight a losing cause the right thing. Perhaps his father, too, was softening. If Saguaro Flower was returned, Cochise would not lose face by saying, "Make peace and survive, Indian brothers."

The reservation was, perhaps, a better alternative than fighting to the death. There were too few Apaches left. Like the buffalo, their numbers and territory grew smaller and smaller with the passing years.

But the old man would die ordering his people to fight, unless he could save face. Getting Saguaro Flower back was probably impossible by now . . .

"I want the soldiers as bounty, and their mounts," Naiche said.

One Who Trades With Enemies translated.

Glidinghawk said, "It shall be done. Some of the soldiers are dead—perhaps all of them by now—but you shall see that they have been destroyed."

It will be the firing squad for me if Washington City finds I have traded soldiers' lives for those of Powell's Army, Glidinghawk thought. *But otherwise we all will die. If any of Hardy's men yet live, I will do them the mercy of killing them. These Chiricahua would torture them for days before letting them die. It must be done.*

"Next, I want the gold the slavers traded the lives of my people for."

"It shall be done."

"But you and your friends will still die, unless you prove your faith by getting my daughter back," Naiche concluded. "I have spoken."

As if to punctuate his words, the sky began to rumble. The Chiricahua looked uneasily to the sky. After many centuries of surviving here, they knew what the ominous sounds meant. The One Who Made All Things was angry.

"We'd better get to high ground," Glidinghawk said, more to himself than anyone else. His words were repeated to Naiche. The Indian barked orders to the warriors attending him. Women scattered to the wickiups, starting to dismantle them.

"There is no time," Glidinghawk said urgently. This time, he meant to be heard. He explained that the hideaway was built on firm, elevated ground, far above the gorge. It might be their safest bet—except that between the freed captives, including a few children, and the braves, there were close to a hundred Chiricahua who needed shelter.

"Take the Omaha along as our hostage," Naiche said. "We will take shelter in the hills."

So, along with women and the few children, Glidinghawk was herded back up into the hills. The Indian ponies were secured inside the corral that once held human beings.

Naiche spoke to the men who were waiting to attack the hideaway. "Wait," he said. "We will not kill them now. If this Omaha and his people can fulfill the bargain he has made, we will let them live. First, we must all survive the storm — except for the soldiers. Those, you may kill."

The braves gathered around and nodded.

It was the way it should be, they understood. Had they been in the desert valleys, rather than in these mountains avenging the wrong done their people, their chances would be slim against the death rains. Perhaps the spirits were with them.

Glidinghawk was sent alone to the hideaway. Neither Naiche nor his hand-picked bodyguards, ten of the biggest, bravest warriors, accompanied him. They had a deal — but they would not trust walking into the camp with Glidinghawk. They knew all too well that the life of a solitary Indian was cheap.

Before letting Glidinghawk go, Naiche told the Omaha, "You and your people have but the blink of an eye to walk out unarmed with the soldiers you will turn over to my braves. If you are not out of there, we will attack to kill all of you."

"We will do as you say," Glidinghawk promised.

He knew that the hideaway was most likely the safest

place to be with the rains that threatened, even now, to pour down from the sky. The adobe dwelling looked as if it had weathered flash floods before. There was no reason for Naiche and the others to let Glidinghawk's people stay there.

Just where they would find safety — assuming the Chiricahua did not change their minds and kill them — he did not know.

Landrum opened the door to him. "Well?"

"Shoot Hardy and the others right now," Glidinghawk said.

Fox was startled so badly his entire body shook.

"It is the kindest way," Glidinghawk said grimly. "We shoot them, or the Apache will torture them, or we are all dead, take your pick."

"And us?" Landrum said.

"We might have a chance. They want it all — soldiers punished, the gold and the slaves back, including Saguaro Flower. That's their deal and I had no choice but to take it. These men," Glidinghawk looked at the four terrified soldiers, "would have been killed anyway, if they ever lived to come to trial."

"Oh God, I can't shoot them," Celia said.

"Hurry, we have no time. We have to come out of here unarmed. That's thunder you hear, and a torrent is going to start any second."

"Please, have mercy. God have mercy," the eighteen-year-old soldier sobbed.

Hardy's face was ashen. He dimly understood. Get shot now, painlessly, or suffer at the hands of the murderous heathen until he begged for the release of death. It was not a great choice.

How did this start? Hardy wondered. *All I wanted was to make some extra money . . . and get rid of Injuns. What was wrong with that? Injuns is just animals.*

A forked tongue of lightning flicked to earth.

"Now," Glidinghawk said urgently.

"I'll shoot them," Landrum said, disgusted as much at himself as at Fox, who had gotten them all into this dilemma. He understood Celia's feelings. He shared them. He did not want to play God.

Moments hung in the air like years.

Landrum's thoughts were these: *If I let Glidinghawk do the shooting, the army will execute him if they ever find out. Maybe I'd stand a chance in court, if the officers at my trial understand what Indian torture is . . . but I wish Celia didn't have to see this.*

Landrum raised his pistol and cocked it.

Hardy hid his face in his hands.

The young man cowered on the floor saying last prayers.

The one named Williams stood paralyzed, and the soldier beside him cursed God, his mother and the army.

Landrum was about to shoot.

The rat-tat-tat of the first large raindrops beat on the roof. Celia turned her head to the wall. Outside, the Apache waited for their prisoners. Landrum squinted his eyes.

"Stop!" Fox said, deadly calm. The second lieutenant raised his pistol and shot. Cordite stung the air. A hole the size of a silver dollar appeared in Hardy's forehead. One.

Williams' damnation curses halted abruptly as he

was hit directly in the front lobe of the brain and he fell heavily to the floor. Two.

The man beside him stared directly into Fox's eyes as Fox squeezed off a third shot. Three.

"Maybe they'll let the young one live," Fox said. "I cannot shoot him. He went along with Williams and Hardy, but he wasn't really part of it."

"Get the bodies and let's go," Glidinghawk said.

He opened the door wide so the Indians could see inside. Landrum threw his weapons outside. Fox added his to the heap, then Celia and Glidinghawk.

Glidinghawk shouldered Hardy's body and heaved it to the earth, so his blood tinged the muddy ground red. The Omaha had not promised live delivery. Landrum picked up another soldier's corpse and hefted it. He walked several paces out in clear view before dumping it.

When the pile of weapons and corpses was on the ground, Glidinghawk led the others to where Naiche was waiting. Fox was retching. The young soldier could barely walk, his fear was so great. Celia's eyes were dry but her heart was heavy. Landrum brought up the rear.

"We have fulfilled the first part of our bargain," Glidinghawk told Naiche. "The rain lashes down already, and all of us, Indian and white, are in danger. What do we do now, wise chief?"

"Some of my braves will guard you in the hills. I must value my own life, because my people have few leaders left. I will take the safety of the shelter. Should you and your people live, you have one more act with which to seal our pact."

Naiche's face was bitter. The son of a chief, chief of

his own small band, he knew why the soldiers had been killed. Out of kindness. And still one lived, a young one. Did they think he was stupid, trying to save one of the blue coats?

Let nature kill them, Naiche thought. *And if they live, their task of getting my daughter back will bring their death.*

"If they die by the hand of One Who Makes All Things, it is nothing to me," Naiche told the braves who had been assigned to Glidinghawk and the others.

Naiche and his closest braves made for the hideaway.

The rains gathered in intensity. A hard wall of silvery water danced to the ground and gathered on top of the startled earth. The parched ground was hard and crusty like rock, and could not absorb it. It gathered in trickles that turned into streams and rivers.

A Chiricahua prodded Landrum with the point of his spear, and the group started to move, fighting against the sudden force of the wind.

There was no safe place to go.

Up was the only alternative. The ground beneath them turned to slippery mud. Celia fell and cut her knee open on a rock. It was almost impossible to stay together.

One of the Indian braves slipped and tumbled into a stream that had not been there seconds before. If he called out, his voice was drowned out by the fury of the storm. The last Glidinghawk saw of him, he was tumbling down the hillside with a torrent of water.

"Up above there," Landrum shouted to Glidinghawk, pointing to an outcropping of rock. "Maybe we can make it if we can get a solid footing and hold on to each other."

Some of their guards had slipped away, seeking their own survival, but a short brave with an antiquated pistol stuck to them like a bad promise. Several more put duty above their own safety.

But as the minutes passed, it was clear that Glidinghawk and Landrum were more or less on their own. There were no clever moves to make. They needed to dig in and wait it out if they could.

In the bright-hot flashes of electricity, Glidinghawk could see Indians trying to flatten themselves to the unstable earth, hanging onto rocks and digging into crevices.

They could only see inches in front of their noses, except when the lightning struck. A group must have been hit—there was a brief, crackling sizzle and the smell of burnt flesh in the air.

No inch of ground was safe or solid.

Sexto's dwelling was weathering the sudden flood, but the ground around it was eroding at a rapid pace. Slightly above and to the left of it, the shack where Landrum and Celia were held prisoner still stood. Its roof was becoming buried in the rushing mudslide, but it looked as if the structure might hold.

Glidinghawk pointed to it.

"We can't go there," Celia yelled. "Please, not there."

They were directly above it, and on high ground, but how long could they hold on until the accumulated rocks and earth crumbled and they were swept away?

Glidinghawk made frantic hand signs to the Apache guard, who seemed to share Celia's fear of the shack built into the mountainside.

Another flash of lightning changed his mind.

It struck close enough so Glidinghawk's fingers tingled with shock. The guard suddenly decided he would allow his prisoners to seek any shelter—it was better than waiting in the open for the forked tongue of death.

Glidinghawk and Landrum started the human chain. Fox, the three guards still with them, the young soldier and Celia joined hands with them. Together, they half slid, half allowed themselves to be swept down.

The momentum of Glidinghawk's body almost pulled them into a gushing river, but he managed to grasp onto a corner of the structure. With effort borne of fear, his grip held.

He pulled Landrum to him, and together they helped the others. Now there was eight of them, including the three Apaches armed with useless pistols. The weapons would never fire, now that the powder was wet.

They had to dig out the door, which was shut solid with mud and debris. Inside, the dead bodies of the slavers already stank of death and putrefication.

At least the bolts of lightning would not touch them here. They were underground—completely underground, if this pileup of rubble and earth continued.

The rain pounded and the mud whooshed by with sickening regularity. Celia sank into Landrum's arms. Fox squatted and waited, staring ahead at black nothingness.

Glidinghawk said, "If we are not buried alive, we might make it."

"Better than being fried," Landrum said as another

clap of thunder deafened them.

It was as dark as night and seemed longer.

Once, the entire shack seemed to sag and shift, but it held. They had to close the doors on the rising level of the rubble and rain.

It was like being in a tomb.

And if by some miracle they survived it, Powell's Army still had an impossible quest ahead of them.

CHAPTER NINETEEN

They survived.

As swiftly as it had started, the rain ceased, leaving destruction in its path. The small stream that was an offshoot of the Black River was swollen with its bounty. New gorges had been etched into the land.

"We will need money for our trip to Sonora," Landrum told Naiche, "or we cannot buy your daughter back, if we can find her."

"That is your problem, white man," Naiche said coldly.

Now that he had discovered Sextos's cache of gold, his mind had turned to buying weapons rather than peace. He wanted to please his father Cochise by sending the strangers for Saguaro Flower, but he wasn't willing to part with any money. Personally, he thought the trip was hopeless.

Landrum and Glidinghawk conferred. "I hid $1500 worth of gold back in the cougar's lair," Landrum said. "If it is still there, maybe we will have a chance."

"I'll go look," Glidinghawk said.

So Gerald made the wet, dangerous descent. By some miracle, the hoard was still there. The cougar was not. Like most of the wildlife in the area, it had been swept away.

But Naiche got wind of the discovery, and demanded half the gold for his own. "We made a bargain, Omaha," he said, "but I will not make it easy for you. Two of my men will go with you. One Who Trades With Enemies will go, because he knows the language and the customs. I will send Rattlesnake also, because he knows how to strike his enemies."

The anger in Naiche's eyes let Glidinghawk know that, whatever happened, Powell's Army was the enemy. They could never be allies. This truce was uneasy — so uneasy that Naiche insisted that Fox, Celia and the young soldier stay with his band as hostages.

"When our mission is complete and we have your daughter, how will we find you, wise chief?" Glidinghawk asked.

"We will find you," Naiche said darkly. He had much to be unhappy about. The flash flood had drowned many of his loyal braves. Fox had reported that soldiers from Fort Apache would come to find the men who were dead, and round the Chiricahua up for the reservation.

The corpses of the soldiers had been washed away in the flood. They would end up as bleached bones scattered over the lowlands, no longer recognizable as ones who had once lived and breathed as men.

Seeing how quickly and finally life ended, Naiche felt a desire for freedom and honor well up in him. Life was too brief to live herded and penned up like heads of beef. Suddenly, the horror of what was happening to his people haunted Naiche more strongly than ever before.

Naiche was concerned about Cochise and the rebel bands scattered in the valleys. The moment he had started thinking of compromising, of going to the reservation and maintaining the army's treaty, the skies had opened up with fury. To Naiche, it was an omen.

But, unlike the white men he dealt with, Naiche was a man of his word. He would let Glidinghawk fulfill his bargain for the lives of the white men and the woman with the flaming red hair.

If the Indian returned with Saguaro Flower, the hostages would live. Otherwise, he would take great pleasure in killing them all slowly — including the woman, since she was somehow tied in with these people. His heart had been hardened; his mind was made up.

Since there were only four of them — Glidinghawk, Landrum and their two Chiricahuan escorts — they made fast time over the desert. They had chosen the best of the horses, and rarely paused to rest.

Naiche's blood brother Rattlesnake chose their route. He had been on many raiding parties south of the border and knew the way. His eyes were as reptilian as his name, and he constantly watched Glidinghawk and Landrum, looking for an excuse to strike them. Naiche had chosen him well: he was firm in his hatred of any man outside his own band.

The desert was spectacular, though they had little time to note it. The destructive flood had receded, causing long dormant seeds to grow and plants to bloom. It was a natural garden unlike any Landrum or Glidinghawk had ever seen. Huge flowers dotted the barren hardpan, their season as brief as it was glorious.

It was a land man could get lost in, Landrum thought. Harsh, yes, but with an unexpected, tough beauty.

The Chiricahua knew this, too. Although garrisons were manned at intervals along their path, they did not see any soldiers. It was deceptive, but the vast reaches of land looked open and free.

They skirted towns, as they got further south, and passed across the border without fanfare. It was a No Man's Land as surely as the Oklahoma Territory was, inhabited only by bandits and raiding Indian bands. These men had no desire to encounter another human being—unless there was some gain in it for them.

Conversation was brief and tense, even between Landrum and Glidinghawk. They had little to say. Celia was on both of their minds constantly. They had to succeed for her sake. Every extra day meant greater danger for her. Naiche and his braves would not wait forever.

So the two of them pushed themselves on the punishing journey. Rattlesnake did not complain, though One Who Trades With Enemies did. "Are you trying to ruin us, Omaha?" he whined in his bastard Spanish. "I will tell Rattlesnake that we must rest tonight."

Glidinghawk was picking up some of the Chiricahuan dialect, though. In faltering words, he managed to take Rattlesnake aside and tell him, "Just as you are loyal to Naiche, so I am loyal to the people I now live with. We must rush like the wind."

Rattlesnake began to have a grudging respect for Glidinghawk and the white man. Landrum was proving himself to be as stoic as an Indian.

During one of their hiatuses from the grueling desert ride, Landrum was laying out his bedroll. He asked for no more in the way of stale water or rations than a Chiricahuan would. The lean, tired man did his part to tether the horses and look out for unwanted intruders.

That night, he had done more than his share. He slumped into his bedroll without looking. A scorpion bit him on the back right through his sweat-soaked shirt.

Landrum yelped once and sat bolt upright. Rattlesnake saw the creature writhing, its stinger imbedded. The Chiricahua leapt forward and beat the scorpion off. He stomped it aside with his moccasin, but it did not die. He took his rifle and slammed the butt end into the ugly creature.

Landrum's face was drawn with pain. Rattlesnake knew grown braves who had sobbed and cried out from a sting like that. The scorpion was almost three inches long. Landrum gritted his teeth and did not cry out, after that first time.

When he was able, though he looked like death with only the scar across his cheek livid and alive, Landrum said in the Apache tongue, "That was a brave thing you did for me."

And later, when the sickness from the poison came over Landrum, he had insisted on riding on south to their destination. It made Rattlesnake wonder, that this white man could learn some words of his language and be as brave as a warrior. Landrum, from then on, was a respected enemy.

Still, Rattlesnake was worried about Sonora. He knew that the Mexican townspeople feared and hated Indians—except as slaves to work their fields, clean their kitchens and warm their beds.

So, once the village was in sight, mostly hovels of mud with a few larger, adobe mansions hidden behind thick walls, Rattlesnake asked, "What must you do now? I hold the gold, and you hold the knowledge of how to get the maiden back. To trust you would be my death at the hands of my people."

This was translated, and Glidinghawk replied, "Landrum and I will go alone to the town, then, and learn what we can. If money is to change hands, we will need to work on a plan. For now, let us go. Give us a day of freedom from your watchful eye. You know that Naiche still holds the sister we hold dear."

Rattlesnake accepted this. He would rather wait in the camp they had made, along with One Who Trades With Enemies. Without money, those two would not go far. Rattlesnake had seen the truth of their concern, had seen the tall one ride on when he was ill.

"Will you give us weapons?" Landrum asked.

Glidinghawk had spent days wondering if they would have to go into Sonora unarmed. He had anticipated it. More and more, it was easy for Glidinghawk to think as the mean-eyed Chiricahua did. A man who was being closed in and suffocated had little use for friends or allies; everyone was truly an enemy to be feared.

"I will give the tall one his own Peacemaker," Rattlesnake decided. "You may have your knife that kills silently."

"Thank you. We will not betray your trust," Glidinghawk said.

"*Ayie*. If you do not return by next sundown, One Who Trades With Enemies and I will hunt you down and kill you. I do not like the villages of Mexico, but I will not return to my people in disgrace."

"I understand," Glidinghawk said. "I have promised we will not flee from you. We both want the same thing."

"No," Rattlesnake said thoughtfully. "I want the death of all who would change this land and those of us it belongs to. But the matter of pleasing Cochise, we are one, though for different reasons."

"We will do our best to release his granddaughter," Glidinghawk said.

Unexpectedly, before they rode off, Rattlesnake added, "May you find success."

CHAPTER TWENTY

As towns go, Sonora had little to recommend it. Crooked, dusty streets smelled of poverty and poor sanitation. The fields were planted but lacked fertility; the crops eked out of this harsh earth, crops such as beans and hard-kerneled corn, were far from lush.

The money in the town, more often than not, came from smuggling and raids on the richer territories to the north. To these peasants, life was cheap and mainly without hope.

Sexto Diaz had made himself into a big man in the town. He had been cruel and ruthless and he brought gold wrested from the hated Americans.

Others of his ilk lived in Sonora also, but none as singleminded as Sexto had been. That did not make the other bandits, thieves and slavers any less deadly, though.

Sometimes, Americans would pass through the town escaping justice. They were dog turds, every one, but mean and fast with their guns.

When they had money to spend they were welcomed

into the cantinas and whorehouses. When they did not, they often tried to get what they needed by force. They were always an unknown quantity, these non-Mexicans who ventured through Sonora.

Landrum could feel the gazes upon him as he and Glidinghawk rode through the crooked, rutted main street. Only the lower half of his face showed beneath his broad-brimmed hat. His pistol was holstered but in plain sight so it glittered in the late afternoon sun.

Glidinghawk had no trouble looking fierce and deadly; none of the softness of civilization was left in him.

Women in long, gathered skirts worn from many washings, their bodies underneath stout and squat, rushed for the safety of adobe houses. A child who had been defecating on the street rushed after his mother and buried himself beneath the folds of her garment.

Men, sleepy from siesta time, scratched themselves and wondered what fresh trouble was riding into their lives. Those who could afford it ambled toward Rosa's Cantina to catch up on the latest gossip.

Landrum reined in his horse. He knew a saloon when he saw one, no matter what they called it down here. There was no hitching post: Most of the people had no money for animals to ride. They were fortunate if they had burros to plow with, rather than themselves.

There was a stunted tree outside the peeling, green-painted building, though. Glidinghawk dismounted first, and tied Landrum's mount alongside his own. He felt rather than saw the sidelong looks of hatred he was receiving.

Together, the two men strode to the open door of the cantina. The sing-song buzz of conversation inside hushed. Landrum's Texas boots made a clomping sound on the earthen floor.

Landrum and Glidinghawk were rough hombres, killers or at the very least rustlers. They were dusty from the trail, but there was something more as well, a hardness in their faces, a toughness in their eyes.

Landrum had some small pocket change; he hoped it would be enough. He had a bad feeling about Sonora. It was like walking into a pack of vultures.

These people had so little — almost as little as the Indians in the Arizona Territory. Except, the Apache there had a way of life that made existence tolerable. Here . . . well, there were no rules unless the strong preying on the weak was a rule.

Glidinghawk's thoughts were similar: *These people have been beaten by the Conquistadors and stomped on by the Americans. They have interbred and lost all roots. What do they care about, except hatred for those who have more than they do? Fear for those who are stronger? And this, too, could be the future of my people. . . .*

There was a plump woman behind a planked bar, presumably Rosa. Aside from her, all the patrons were men. There were no saloon girls or prostitutes. Those operated out of a different establishment.

The men looked foreign and sly. They huddled at tables whispering in Spanish, staring into their shots of tequila. Their reception was wary.

Landrum plunked some change in front of the woman. Suddenly, his throat was very dry. "See if they have any beer, Glidinghawk," he said.

"*Dos cervezas,*" Glidinghawk ordered.

This was one establishment where nobody was about to say, "We don't serve Indians." The Mexicans were well aware of Landrum's loaded Peacemaker. More than one envied the gun.

The woman slid the beers across the counter. Landrum drank deeply, listening for any movement behind him. He edged over to a table with a good view of the door and sat, his one hand close to his side, just in case.

Because Glidinghawk was proficient in Spanish, he did the talking before joining Landrum. He asked, "Could you tell me where we can find the house of Señora Diaz?"

Rosa stammered, "No, we have no Diaz here in Sonora. She does not live here."

Landrum's mouth was foamy from the slug of beer he had just downed. It tasted cool and good. He took one more big gulp before reaching for his gun.

An old man at the next table said, "That one, that Rosa, she knows nothing. Perhaps you could give me some coins, and I can remember where the señora lives."

"Bribery would be too easy, dammit," Landrum said, reaching for the Peacemaker.

"But I will tell you because I am friends with the Americanos, no? She lives in the big house behind the garden wall, on the road south. You cannot miss it. Heh?"

His friends chorused that the tall man with the gun could not miss it. Landrum chugged the rest of his beer as he rose to leave. Glidinghawk was already halfway to the door. He did not care for beer.

"*Gracias,*" Landrum said gruffly, waving his pistol.

"From what Jaime said, Carmen Diaz will be overjoyed about her husband's death," Glidinghawk said. "Diaz beat her all the time, her brother told me. I hope she knows who bought Saguaro Flower."

"So do I. I want to get out of here. I can't explain it, but I feel a lot safer with Rattlesnake than I do with these people."

"Yes. If they think we have money, they will shoot us in a minute and ask questions later. We are so conspicuous riding in like this."

"Conspicu—what?" What the hell are you talking about?"

"We stand out like pigs in a poke," Glidinghawk said. "So far, this is too easy. We ride into town like tough guys and everybody gets out of our way."

"Not everybody!" Landrum exclaimed, drawing and firing.

A man dodged behind the house they were approaching. It was the Diaz house, and much larger than its neighbors. Landrum had not intended to hit the man who had poked his nose—and a weapon—out from behind a wall, only to scare him. Landrum was thoroughly spooked, and his nervousness showed.

"Carmen Diaz!" Glidinghawk shouted.

A heart-shaped face appeared briefly at a window.

"I have news from your brother Jaime. I come from the Gila Mountains with a message for you."

The man Landrum had frightened appeared out in the open carrying a rifle of ancient vintage. It was pointed straight at Landrum's heart. He was an old man, stooped and grizzled. The newer, shinier pistol Landrum was pointing at the old man did not daunt him. The expression across his wizened face was that of an elder banty rooster.

"You hurt my daughter, I will kill you," the old man said.

"You do not look fast enough, old man," Glidinghawk said, "but we come with news, not to harm Señora Diaz."

The situation bordered on the comic. Landrum covered the old man who covered him as the three of them made their way to the house. Carmen was waiting.

"Let's make this fast," Landrum said.

"That suits me," Glidinghawk said, slipping into Spanish. "We have little time. I knew your brother Jaime, who told me of your problems. Sexto Diaz is dead."

Carmen's face came alive—and it was not with grief. The old man cackled gleefully. "The bastard got what he deserved. And his man, Jose? Is he still alive?"

"They are all dead," Glidinghawk said.

"Jaime?" Carmen asked with a sob.

The joy she had shown a moment before became grief. "He was killed also," Glidinghawk said. Then he lied. "He was brave and helped defeat Sexto so you could be free. He asked me to tell you to light a candle for him at the church."

The woman cried. The old man shrank more into himself, as if life had finally overwhelmed him, after giving him a moment's happiness. But he was old and his moods were mercurial.

"Ask about the Apache girl now," Landrum urged. "We don't have time to be polite."

"We traveled far to bring this news," Glidinghawk said, "But we need something from you."

"No," the old man said stubbornly. "We are poor, we have nothing, we have suffered, and now you want—"

"Stop, father," Carmen said. "What would you have from me? If you come for Sexto's riches, go ask that whore Bonita!"

"It is not money we seek," Glidinghawk said. "On the last trip Sexto made to Sonora, he had with him a young Apache maiden, a beautiful Indian girl named Saguaro Flower. She is not meant to be a slave. In her land, she is daughter of a chief. We must find her. Can you tell us where she is?"

"I remember that one," the old man said. "The virgin. She was sold to Manuel Rodriguez, an old goat with many pesos. He is a big landowner, and has many peons under him. To get her away from him will not be easy."

The old man's tongue loosened considerably when he learned they were not after his daughter's money. His grief for his weak-willed son was short-lived.

He told Glidinghawk and Landrum where the estate of Rodriguez was, and how many men guarded it. He seemed to take a perverse pleasure in the thought that his rich neighbor might be bested.

Disgusted, Landrum said, "Have we heard enough? These people leave a bad taste in my mouth."

Finally, after going over details one more time, Glidinghawk said, "All right. Let's leave the happy widow. We will have to do without the Chiricahuas' help—and we have to move fast."

"You think Rattlesnake and One Who Trades With Enemies will not come across with the money? For God's sake, they can keep an eye on us. Let's just ride in and buy the girl back."

"It's not that easy," Glidinghawk said. "Rodriguez is not about to let her go. Besides, unless you hadn't noticed, that old man and his daughter will be right over to the old goat's house selling the same information they just gave us."

"I told you I didn't like this town. Anything else I should know?"

"Yes. Rodriguez is the richest man in town. He employs several men to guard his hacienda, and all of them are tough," Glidinghawk said.

"So what do you suggest?"

"We have no choice. We break in and steal her back."

"Damn. I wish you had a revolver," Landrum said.

"You do? Hell, I wish I was two hundred miles away. Rodriguez' chief honcho is supposed to be a wrestler as well as a marksman, built like a bull."

"And stupid. Please tell me he is stupid," Landrum said.

"We'll find out," Glidinghawk suggested. "Fire a shot and see what happens."

"Now that's stupid."

"Any better ideas?"

"Let's go over the wall and take them by surprise."

Glidinghawk looked at the high barrier with broken glass embedded in the top. "You know what *cojones* are?" he whispered to Landrum. "I value mine. Unless you have any great ideas on how we get over it without getting cut up."

"All it takes is guts and no sense," Landrum said. "I'm more worried about those barking dogs. On the wall, here's the way we do it. When it gets darker, we bring our horses right up to the outside of the wall. Then we put a saddle across the hump of the wall, over the broken glass, and we can slide over clean and easy. We might get shot and dog-bit, but we'll still have our *cojones*."

Glidinghawk nodded. "You know, it might work. I like your devious mind. The US Army will appreciate how well we treat their saddle. How are you at killing dogs?"

It went well, almost without hitch. Glidinghawk topped the wall and found himself on the other side, sliding right into the jaws of a snarling dog. Glidinghawk did not know what kind it was; he didn't want to know. It was large and mean and made a lot of noise — until the Omaha's knife stabbed it in the heart.

By the time the second dog was on top of him, Landrum had slid down and fired a shot at it.

"Let's find a good place to ambush the guards. They should be here any second after that noise," Landrum said.

They ran silently for the shadows outside the main entrance of the hacienda and waited.

Not long before, the father of Carmen had come visiting, the father-in-law of Sexto, but he had not brought a warning. Instead, he had gossiped and brought a bottle of brandy. He had asked how Manuel was enjoying his new concubine.

Rodriguez did not turn the man away, but he was impatient. Tonight, he had promised himself, all would be well with his love life.

Manuel had boasted and lied, telling the other old man how young, tender flesh made his manhood stand up night after night. He lied so much he began to believe his own stories, especially after the level in the brandy bottle got low.

Now, climbing the stairs to where the beautiful squaw awaited him, Manuel knew his lie, and it brought him anger. Saguaro Flower was a prize he had paid dearly for, but if she could not revive his wilted manhood tonight, he would kill her. She was his. It was his right.

He heard the barking of his dogs, a single shot, and his men Fidel and Paulo yelling. Let them take care of it. He paid them dearly enough.

Paulo was the first one outside, since he was younger and his status was low. He was thinking of payday and how cheap the old bastard Rodriquez was. Still, he would have enough to buy mesa flour and beans for his mother, and get drunk and buy a woman.

Life was hard but tolerable, he thought as his ended. Glidinghawk's knife cut it short in the space of a heartbeat. His body was dragged out of sight.

"There should be only one more, the real killer, and the servants. Let's hope they are not trusted with guns," Glidinghawk whispered.

"I hope the other one is as careless," Landrum said

grimly, edging along the outside wall of the hacienda looking for a way in, just in case.

The trouble was, the windows were all barred.

If the second bodyguard did not come out, they would have to storm the main entrance. Breathing deeply, trying to keep their taut nerves calm, they waited in the purplish shadows.

An immense form appeared at the door. Fidel. His belly was rounded and massive, but muscular. He was tall for a Mexican, perhaps an offshoot of the American bandits who spread their seed south of the border. His thighs were like tree trunks and his thick, hairy arms were weapons. He had a pistol in his ham-sized fist.

"Paulo?" he shouted. "You yellow-bellied piece of manure, where are you?"

Landrum and Glidinghawk exchanged one brief, questioning glance. Landrum nodded almost imperceptibly. Glidinghawk called in his Spanish, "Pss. From here, you can see the old man and the squaw. What a woman for a shriveled up old goat!"

Reassured, a laugh rumbled from deep in Fidel's ample belly. "This I must see. But what was the trouble? The old man grows more afraid every day."

"I saw a boy running outside the wall," Glidinghawk lied. He tried to keep his voice muffled. Maybe he was going too far.

But Fidel had wondered about the squaw. His manhood stiffened with curiosity. He ambled out toward Glidinghawk waiting in the shadow below the old man's window.

The man was too big, too heavily sheathed with

muscle. Landrum did not consult with Glidinghawk; he knew the revolver was a far better weapon than a knife. Sticking a knife in Fidel would be like sticking a hog with a toothpick.

When Fidel came within range, Landrum squeezed off a shot. The big man roared and bellowed. He kept walking, his gun arm extended. He shot crookedly, in reflex, and fell heavily to the ground. His last thought was: *I want to watch the old skinflint fail with the woman. I will rape her myself one of these days. . . .*

"It's been too easy," Landrum said, gazing down at the dead man.

Then the two men looked at the invitation of the open hacienda door. They looked from side and behind them. They heard a rustling from within, and the shriek of an Indian girl.

Landrum brandished the Peacemaker, Glidinghawk held his knife with the blade ready, and they moved, swift as an avenging force.

The opulent interior of the hacienda was surprising after what they had seen of Sonora. No wonder the poor people hated the aging landowner. Servants scattered and hid, none brave enough to challenge the two fierce-looking men.

Upstairs, Rodriguez was at the peak of his frustration. He was holding a whip in his right hand and his limp member in his left hand when Landrum shot him through the back.

Saguaro Flower, naked and vulnerable, lay tied to the old man's bed. When she saw Glidinghawk's strong, Indian face, she did not relax. After the last few weeks, she could not conceive of release. She grabbed for Glidinghawk's knife. She wanted to plunge it into her own heart.

"No, Chiricahuan woman. I take you back to your people. Your father Naiche and your grandfather Cochise await you. Come . . ."

CHAPTER TWENTY-ONE

Celia, Fox, Landrum and Glidinghawk were forced to walk the last miles to Fort Apache.

"You have returned what was rightfully ours," Naiche told them sternly. "I return the white woman and the man called Fox to you unharmed. The animals and gold are little enough for us to keep. Tell the soldiers that next time they try to round us up, we will fight."

With that, the Chiricahuan chief departed. He would go back to his father and daughter further south. They were in a new, semi-permanent camp, more deeply hidden than the last one. The soldiers would find them, but it would take time.

Fox walked behind the others. His ragged Mexican costume embarrassed him greatly. "How can I face the officers?" he mumbled.

Landrum did not reply. His mouth was set in a harsh line. He was not angry with Fox. He understood that the younger man was still stunned from seeing Chiricahuans torture the soldier he had spared.

It was ironic. The boy would have been far better off shot by Fox's hand. Fox had learned that life was not simple. It did not run by West Point rules. It was easier, now, to worry about being out of uniform than to remember.

Glidinghawk fell back and said to Fox, "For the official record, Sexto Diaz and his men killed the soldiers."

"Why not the Indians? They were responsible," Fox said.

"No, those soldiers were responsible for their own deaths. There is no cause to stir up further trouble. There is too much hatred already."

Fox was silent. When they paused to drink deeply from the canteens they had been provided with, he announced to all of them, "I will go along with whatever you want to tell them at Fort Apache. But I am going to make an unofficial report to Amos Powell and tell him everything. I think he might want me to resign."

Landrum and Celia were huddled together so their legs touched. Glidinghawk stood alone, looking out at the vast reaches of land.

"As you wish," Landrum finally said. He knew he spoke for the three of them. "But talk with Powell honestly. Tell him that we would still like you on our team. Tell him that you have learned how difficult our job is, and you have made difficult decisions. We have grown to respect you."

"Yes," Glidinghawk added. "And if you resign, they might give us a liaison officer right out of West Point."

Fox smiled weakly.

There was nothing more to say, so they walked in silence until the first army sentry spotted them. They were weary and dusty and defeated. There were no jokes in them, no bright anticipation of baths and regular meals and the comforts of strong drink.

As three armed soldiers rode out to escort them the final hundred yards to the army garrison, there was nothing but the dulled sorrow for a mission that they never could have succeeded at, and the knowledge of bitterness in a bitter land.

Maybe in the night, the cactus flowers would bloom.

THE UNTAMED WEST
brought to you by Zebra Books

THE LAST MOUNTAIN MAN (1480, $2.25)
by William W. Johnstone

He rode out West looking for the men who murdered his father and brother. When an old mountain man taught him how to kill a man a hundred different ways from Sunday, he knew he'd make sure they all remembered . . . THE LAST MOUNTAIN MAN.

SAN LOMAH SHOOTOUT (1853, $2.50)
by Doyle Trent

Jim Kinslow didn't even own a gun, but a group of hardcases tried to turn him into buzzard meat. There was only one way to find out why anybody would want to stretch his hide out to dry, and that was to strap on a borrowed six-gun and ride to death or glory.

TOMBSTONE LODE (1915, $2.95)
by Doyle Trent

When the Josey mine caved in on Buckshot Dobbs, he left behind a rich vein of Colorado gold—but no will. James Alexander, hired to investigate Buckshot's self-proclaimed blood relations learns too soon that he has one more chance to solve the mystery and save his skin or become another victim of TOMBSTONE LODE.

GALLOWS RIDERS (1934, $2.50)
by Mark K. Roberts

When Stark and his killer-dogs reached Colby, all it took was a little muscle and some well-placed slugs to run roughshod over the small town—until the avenging stranger stepped out of the shadows for one last bloody showdown.

DEVIL WIRE (1937, $2.50)
by Cameron Judd

They came by night, striking terror into the hearts of the settlers. The message was clear: Get rid of the devil wire or the land would turn red with fencestringer blood. It was the beginning of a brutal range war.

Available wherever paperbacks are sold, or order direct from the Publisher. Send cover price plus 50¢ per copy for mailing and handling to Zebra Books, Dept. 2073, 475 Park Avenue South, New York, N.Y. 10016. Residents of New York, New Jersey and Pennsylvania must include sales tax. DO NOT SEND CASH.

BEST OF THE WEST
from Zebra Books

BROTHER WOLF (1728, $2.95)
by Dan Parkinson
Only two men could help Lattimer run down the sheriff's killers—a stranger named Stillwell and an Apache who was as deadly with a Colt as he was with a knife. One of them would see justice done—from the muzzle of a six-gun.

CALAMITY TRAIL (1663, $2.95)
by Dan Parkinson
Charles Henry Clayton fled to the west to make his fortune, get married and settle down to a peaceful life. But the situation demanded that he strap on a six-gun and ride toward a showdown of gunpowder and blood that would send him galloping off to either death or glory on the . . . *Calamity Trail*.

THUNDERLAND (1991, $3.50)
by Dan Parkinson
Men were suddenly dying all around Jonathan, and he needed to know why—before he became the next bloody victim of the ancient sword that would shape the future of the Texas frontier.

APACHE GOLD (1899, $2.95)
by Mark K. Roberts & Patrick E. Andrews
Chief Halcon burned with a fierce hatred for the pony soldiers that rode from Fort Dawson, and vowed to take the scalp of every round-eye in the territory. Sergeant O'Callan must ride to glory or death for peace on the new frontier.

OKLAHOMA SHOWDOWN (1961, $2.25)
by Patrick E. Andrews
When Dace chose the code of lawman over an old friendship, he knew he might have to use his Colt .45 to back up his choice. Because a meeting between good friends who'd ended up on different sides of the law as sure to be one blazing hellfire.

Available wherever paperbacks are sold, or order direct from the Publisher. Send cover price plus 50¢ per copy for mailing and handling to Zebra Books, Dept. 2073, 475 Park Avenue South, New York, N.Y. 10016. Residents of New York, New Jersey and Pennsylvania must include sales tax. DO NOT SEND CASH.

SPINE TINGLING HORROR
from Zebra Books

CHILD'S PLAY (1719, $3.50)
by Andrew Neiderman
From the day the foster children arrived, they looked up to Alex. But soon they began to act like him — right down to the icy sarcasm, terrifying smiles and evil gleams in their eyes. Oh yes, they'd do anything to please Alex.

THE DOLL (1788, $3.50)
by Josh Webster
When Gretchen cradled the doll in her arms, it told her things — secret, evil things that her sister Mary could never know about. For it hated Mary just as she did. And it knew how to get back at Mary . . . forever.

DEW CLAWS (1808, $3.50)
by Stephen Gresham
The memories Jonathan had of his Uncle and three brothers being sucked into the fetid mud of the Night Horse Swamp were starting to fade . . . only to return again. It had taken everything he loved. And now it had come back — for him.

TOYS IN THE ATTIC (1862, $3.95)
by Daniel Ransom
Brian's best friend Davey had disappeared and already his clothes and comic books had vanished — as if Davey never existed. Somebody was playing a deadly game — and now it was Brian's turn . . .

THE ALCHEMIST (1865, $3.95)
by Les Whitten
Of course, it was only a hobby. No harm in that. The small alchemical furnace in the basement could hardly invite suspicion. After all, Martin was a quiet, government worker with a dead-end desk job. . . . Or was he?

Available wherever paperbacks are sold, or order direct from the Publisher. Send cover price plus 50¢ per copy for mailing and handling to Zebra Books, Dept. 2073, 475 Park Avenue South, New York, N.Y. 10016. Residents of New York, New Jersey and Pennsylvania must include sales tax. DO NOT SEND CASH.

THRILLING FICTION
From Zebra Books

ANVIL (1792, $3.50)
by Peter Leslie
The German defenders have their orders: "The Führer counts on you to fight to the last man." But each man of the Allied force of "Operation Anvil" has his orders too: smash the Nazi war machine and either live in freedom or die in its name!

DAGGER (1399, $3.50)
by William Mason
The President needs his help, but the CIA wants him dead. And for Dagger—war hero, survival expert, ladies man and mercenary extraordinaire—it will be a game played for keeps.

EAGLE DOWN (1644, $3.75)
by William Mason
To Western eyes, the Russian Bear appears to be in hibernation—but half a world away, a plot is unfolding that will unleash its awesome, deadly power. When the Russian Bear rises up, God help the Eagle!

THE OASIS PROJECT (1296, $3.50)
by David Stuart Arthur
The President had a plan—a plan that by all rights should not exist. And it would be carried out by the ASP, a second generation space shuttle that would transport the laser weapons into position—before the Red Tide hit U.S. shores.

Available wherever paperbacks are sold, or order direct from the Publisher. Send cover price plus 50¢ per copy for mailing and handling to Zebra Books, Dept. 2073, 475 Park Avenue South, New York, N.Y. 10016. Residents of New York, New Jersey and Pennsylvania must include sales tax. DO NOT SEND CASH.

NIGHT AMBUSH

Gerald Glidinghawk grabbed Devil by the neck and swung around to the other side, so that both he and Celia were protected by the sorrel's proud, arched neck.

He heard the approaching Apache pony whinny and then the battle cry of the lone Chiricahua.

He pressed closer to Celia's limp body. He had no weapon. It was not easy to stand there in the dark night, helpless, fighting the quivering horse, the weight of the woman he wanted more than anything to save, and the overwhelming fear of his own death.

And then the sudden crack of a rifle shot exploded in his ears.

VISIT THE WILD WEST
with Zebra Books

SPIRIT WARRIOR (1795, $2.50)
by G. Clifton Wisler

The only settler to survive the savage Indian attack was a little boy. Although raised as a red man, every man was his enemy when the two worlds clashed — but he vowed no man would be his equal.

IRON HEART (1736, $2.25)
by Walt Denver

Orphaned by an Indian raid, Ben vowed he'd never rest until he'd brought death to the Arapahoes. And it wasn't long before they came to fear the rider of vengeance they called . . . *Iron Heart*.

THE DEVIL'S BAND (1903, $2.25)
by Robert McCaig

For Pinkerton detective Justin Lark, the next assignment was the most dangerous of his career. To save his beautiful young client's sisters and brother, he had to face the meanest collection of hardcases he had ever seen.

KANSAS BLOOD (1775, $2.50)
by Jay Mitchell

The Barstow Gang put a bullet in Toby Markham, but they didn't kill him. And when the Barstow's threatened a young girl named Lonnie, Toby was finished with running and ready to start killing.

SAVAGE TRAIL (1594, $2.25)
by James Persak

Bear Paw seemed like a harmless old Indian — until he stole the nine-year-old son of a wealthy rancher. In the weeks of brutal fighting the guns of the White Eyes would clash with the ancient power of the red man.

Available wherever paperbacks are sold, or order direct from the Publisher. Send cover price plus 50¢ per copy for mailing and handling to Zebra Books, Dept. 2073, 475 Park Avenue South, New York, N.Y. 10016. Residents of New York, New Jersey and Pennsylvania must include sales tax. DO NOT SEND CASH.